"I suppose it wouldn't do to advertise that there's a beautiful brunette living here, instead of a witch?" Hank asked.

"Get your eyes checked, Hank. Your son just about fainted when he got his first look at the real me," Sally said.

He studied her until she blushed. "Willie thought you were going to put a hex on him. You could have been Miss America and he wouldn't have noticed."

She smiled at that, but she had to warn him. "Hank, when Willie fell out of that tree, I had just gotten up from a nap. I don't sleep well. I don't wake up pretty. For the first ten minutes, wrinkled and ugly just about says it."

He looked skeptical and not a bit bothered. "Are you afraid I'll run screaming if you look less than gorgeous the morning after I make love to you?" he asked, picturing her mussed hair and swollen lips after a night of pleasure.

Her breath caught at his words, and when he crossed the room to pull her into his arms, she couldn't speak.

"You need to get this straight, Sally. I don't care what you've suckered the people in town into believing about you. This is about us. And I intend to stick around and figure out why you've got me twisted inside out."

"Don't talk like that," she said softly. "You're scaring me."

He shook his head. "You don't scare that easily. You're just nervous because you haven't done this in a while. Trust me," he urged, his mouth a breath from hers. "This is going to knock your socks off."

She curled her hands around his neck, and murmured in a husky voice, "I'm not wearing any socks. . . ."

WHAT ARE *LOVESWEPT* ROMANCES?

They are stories of true romance and touching emotion. We believe those two very important ingredients are constants in our highly sensual and very believable stories in the *LOVESWEPT* line. Our goal is to give you, the reader, stories of consistently high quality that may sometimes make you laugh, sometimes make you cry, but are always fresh and creative and contain many delightful surprises within their pages.

Most romance fans read an enormous number of books. Those they truly love, they keep. Others may be traded with friends and soon forgotten. We hope that each *LOVESWEPT* romance will be a treasure—a "keeper." We will always try to publish

LOVE STORIES YOU'LL NEVER FORGET
BY AUTHORS YOU'LL ALWAYS REMEMBER

The Editors

523

Victoria Leigh
Bewitched

BANTAM BOOKS
NEW YORK · TORONTO · LONDON · SYDNEY · AUCKLAND

BEWITCHED

A Bantam Book / February 1992

If you would be interested in receiving protective vinyl
covers for your Loveswept books, please write to this address
for information:

Loveswept
Bantam Books
P.O. Box 985
Hicksville, NY 11802

ISBN 0-553-44137-X

Published simultaneously in the United States and Canada

PRINTED IN THE UNITED STATES OF AMERICA

OPM   0 9 8 7 6 5 4 3 2 1

For Peter,
a rabbit with impeccable taste
in the choice of guardians.

Prologue

William Alton took a deep breath and wondered, not for the first time in his life, if he was going to live through the next few minutes.

He had his doubts.

When he'd first been given the mission, it hadn't sounded so bad. But now, with the objective in view and nothing left but the final stages of execution, his nerves were taut with apprehension.

If he was caught, there would be no mercy. His skin crawled as he considered what that meant. He didn't like the feeling, not one little bit.

He knew he was being watched. He'd taken that for granted, never once imagining they'd give him such a task and deny themselves the satisfaction of watching him perform. Even now, with all of his senses focused on the house across the lane, he could feel the eyes at his back. Moving his head a fraction, he glanced at the fallen cottonwood behind him—the only obvious cover in the forest. He couldn't see them, but he knew they were there.

If he didn't go through with it, there would be no mercy. There was no going back.

His camouflage was a thick stand of aspen, their

leaves a rich green from the hot summer sun. He stood poised within their protection, remembering all the other times he'd been this close to the edge . . . reminding himself that he'd always survived.

He stared at the house and tried to keep his fears in proportion. Doc Savage wouldn't be afraid, he told himself. The hero of the spine-tingling adventure stories to which Willie was currently addicted, Doc Savage was everything Willie wanted to be. Brave and strong and honorable. He fought spies and went on missions and did all those things an eleven-year-old boy found unbelievably exciting.

Willie liked to pretend he was Doc's partner. In perilous situations—like this one—he tended to talk and think like his hero. His eyes narrowed, and he studied his objective for the last time.

The crab-apple tree.

Situated in the garden beside the cottage, it looked innocent enough. There were no real obstacles to keep him from the tree, just a low stone wall that he knew he could slip across.

His mission was to climb the tree and steal a bucketful of apples. His buddies, safely hidden in the forest behind him, had dared him to do it. They needed apples for ammunition, they'd said. Crab apples were the best, and this was the only crab-apple tree in all of Oakville.

If he succeeded, they'd show him the fort they'd built last summer in O'Connor's woods. Willie had heard about the fort all year, but he'd never got to know the boys who'd built it until recently. They were older, in the next grade at school.

This was a test. The apples were his ticket to the fort. He took a deep breath and wondered if it was worth it. He was afraid, and he didn't want to be. Doc Savage wouldn't be afraid, he told himself.

But then, Doc Savage had never met Mad

Sally . . . and it was *her* tree. His breathing quickened as bits of stories flashed through his mind, terrifying tales of the woman who lived in the house at the end of Blossom Lane.

She was mad. She was crazy. She was a witch. Everyone knew it and stayed away. Or she chased them away if they got too close. There were enough of those stories to fill a book, a very scary book. Willie wished he were anywhere but there, and almost gave in to the temptation to run back into the woods.

But he didn't. His new buddies would laugh and call him chicken. That would never do. Doc Savage wouldn't run, so neither would he. He watched the house for signs of life, but saw nothing. Heartened, he manfully thrust aside his fears. It was time.

Willie broke cover and ran all hunched over across the patch of asphalt that served as a road, the tin pail swinging in his hand. Without taking his gaze off the house, he scrambled over the low stone wall that surrounded the garden and was soon shimmying up the tree.

His heart beat loudly against his chest, but he paid no attention. He'd taken the first step; the rest would be easy. Perching precariously on a low branch, he grabbed for the closest apples and frantically began to fill his pail.

A terrifying scream pierced the air. The loud, high-pitched wail ripped up and down his spine, stealing his nerve—and his balance. Too late, he grasped for a handhold and found only air.

He fell, hard, on his back.

He was going to die. Willie knew it, because he couldn't breathe. He closed his eyes and prayed Mad Sally wouldn't get him first.

He was thinking that Doc Savage was going to have to find another partner when his lungs began to fill with air. He took one deep breath, then another, and was beginning to wonder if his buddies were going to rescue him, when he heard a door slam.

Mad Sally! Willie's limbs froze in terror, and he kept his eyes squeezed shut. Maybe, if he stayed real still, she wouldn't see him. The blood pounded in his ears as he lay there, helplessly awaiting his fate.

He felt rather than heard her approach, the brush of cloth on his arm, the slight movement of the air that stirred with her arrival. Willie held his breath, afraid to move . . . afraid to look.

"Are you hurt?"

The soft voice surprised him, and he thought fleetingly that his worst fears hadn't come true at all. But then he opened his eyes, and his hopes crashed. For the first time in his life he was face to face with the woman called Mad Sally.

There could be no mistake who it was. Her face was all squashed and wrinkled, and her hair stuck out all over. It was her eyes, though, that scared him the most. Red-rimmed and almost colorless, they reminded him of the clearie marbles he had in his pocket.

With eyes like those, she had to be a witch.

He screamed.

Mad Sally lifted a hand toward him, and he knew she was going to do something dreadful, like put a hex on him. Or turn him into a frog.

He recoiled from her touch. She appeared to have second thoughts, and he allowed himself a relieved swallow when she sat back on her heels. Then she began talking, but Willie was too busy trying to figure out how to escape to pay attention.

When she stood up and hurried back to the cottage, he realized he had his chance. He rolled to his feet, ran across the few yards of grass, and leaped over the low wall. Then, without worrying about how it looked to his buddies in the forest, he sped down Blossom Lane to safety.

He didn't even look over his shoulder. It wasn't worth the risk.

In the hazy sunshine of that late August afternoon

Mad Sally paused with her hand on the door and turned to watch the flight of the boy. She just stood there, watching, not moving, long after he disappeared from sight.

Then she smiled, a gentle, amused smile.

One

"Amazing recovery," Sally said aloud, and blew out a long breath to release the tension of the last few minutes. It had been quite a scare, seeing the boy fall and not knowing if he'd been injured or if he was just scared.

She grimaced. "Terrified is more like it, Sally girl," she said. Her gaze darted back to the tree, where she discovered a bucket of apples spilling onto the grass. "I wonder how long it will be before he remembers the bucket?" She shrugged. "Remembering and doing something about retrieving it are two entirely different things. I bet he'll chalk it off as a minor loss compared to what might have happened."

Returning to the tree, she knelt beside the bucket and carefully piled the dozen or so apples into her skirt. Making a modest cache of them at about thigh level—high enough not to drop any but low enough for her skirt to cover the essentials—she hooked the pail under one finger and carried it over to where a white picket gate opened onto the lane. She leaned over the gate and put the tin bucket on the ground in plain view. It was the same place she'd left various odds and ends that had ended up in her garden over the years. Sometimes the owners sneaked back to retrieve their missing property. Sometimes they didn't.

She had quite a collection of items dropped by children she'd caught trespassing.

"I really doubt I'll see that little boy again," Sally said. "He looked ready to jump out of his skin." The pang of guilt that should have come with that knowledge had long since been reduced to an insignificant twinge. She'd made the choice between guilt and privacy.

"Falling out of the tree probably scared him as much as anything," she added, but her words didn't carry any real conviction. He'd been frightened of her, pure and simple. She turned to walk back to her cottage, avoiding the cement sidewalk in favor of the soft, cool grass beside it.

She pushed open the front door and spotted the hooded cloak hanging on the coat tree. Now she was *really* puzzled about what had frightened the boy. For nearly five years she'd combined the ghostly potential of the cloak with flailing arms and melodramatic boos and moans to drive trespassers from her garden. It had worked brilliantly, although the challenge of stealing apples and not getting caught by Mad Sally still attracted an occasional misguided adolescent.

She wondered if she should feel just a bit self-conscious. She hadn't even used any props, and the boy had been terrified. Perhaps the theatrics she'd always relied upon were unnecessary. All she had to do was be herself.

Then she caught a glimpse of something genuinely frightful in the mirror beside the coat tree and let out an appreciative cackle. Her reflection was ghastly. A clump of hair was sticking almost straight up at the crown of her head. On one side of her face the shoulder-length dark brown mane was smashed inelegantly in front of her ear, and against her other cheek was a fuzzy confusion of hair that didn't appear to share any common direction. Her porcelain-toned skin was riddled with red creases and wrinkles, and her gray-blue eyes appeared lighter than ever, thanks to the rims of red that circled them.

She looked pretty much the way she always did after sleeping—a wreck. Sally had never understood how some women could wake up looking fresh and beautiful, while she invariably resembled something that crawled out from under a rock. Perhaps it was because she was such a hard sleeper—when she managed to sleep. With the insomnia that plagued her at night, daytime naps were sometimes the only rest she got.

Night or day, though, she always woke up looking the same—frightful. The only saving grace was that with the help of a brush and about ten minutes' time, her appearance would improve significantly. Creases, unnatural wrinkles, and puffiness would disappear, her hair would resume its disciplined, almost straight fall to her shoulders, and she'd suddenly be presentable.

Until then, it was better if she didn't look into any mirrors.

She laughed. "No wonder he ran! If *I* could run away from this reflection, I'd be in the next state by now."

Sally continued talking as she wandered down the long hallway that led to the kitchen, saying hello to the flowering African violets that huddled beneath the warmth of the grow light. "It's a lovely day outside," she said, smiling encouragingly as she stopped to pat a velvety leaf of each plant. "If you'd only remind me not to leave you out all night, you could get some fresh air."

The violets showed no enthusiasm for the excursion, and Sally decided it was just as well. While the August afternoons in the Colorado foothills were pleasantly warm, the evenings were definitely on the chilly side. The last time she'd taken her delicate babies outside, it had been past midnight before she'd remembered them and they'd all but frozen.

She'd insisted that 50 degrees was far from freezing, but they'd been adamant about staying indoors ever since. With an extra pat for her favorite—the one with dark lavender blooms—Sally continued down the hall. She ducked into the tiny bathroom and grabbed a brush, dragging it through her hair as she continued toward the kitchen with her load of apples. Throwing the brush down after only a minimum number of strokes, she opened her skirt and allowed the apples to fall gently into the sink.

"I'll wash you later," she told them. "And tomorrow, we'll have to discuss how you feel about crab-apple jelly—although I have to warn you that I like it a lot."

Sally didn't hear the apples if they did in fact reply. The hearing loss she'd suffered in an explosion five years earlier had left her essentially deaf to all but the loudest of sounds. And because she didn't wear her hearing aids unless there was a reason, most of life's little noises passed her by.

Humming now, she left the apples to their own thoughts and crossed the kitchen to the room at the far end that served as her office. She opened the door, which was usually kept closed against her pet rabbit. Raspberry had a passion for nibbling on paper, and Sally had stacks of it in the small room that also housed a computer and fax machine. Not that she minded when the rabbit attacked the newspaper or other quasi-edibles, but Sally's professional standards required that she prevent such rodentlike signatures from appearing on the manuscripts entrusted into her keeping.

She automatically stepped over a box of paper that she kept meaning to unload into the storage cabinet and picked up a manuscript from the top of the stack on her desk. A couple of seconds later, she'd located a pencil and her reading glasses. Shifting the load onto one hip, she returned to the kitchen and one-handedly filled a glass with ice water. Equipped for work, she sauntered back down the hallway to the front room.

And she remembered the nightmare.

It hit her the moment she saw the wicker sofa, its cushions bunched and wrinkled from her troubled sleep. Slowing her pace to accommodate the sudden tightening of her nerves, Sally returned in her mind to where she'd been split seconds before the excitement outdoors.

"I'd forgotten," she said softly. "The boy. He made me forget." She forced herself to sit down in the chair where she did the majority of her work, her gaze locked on the sofa. With measured care she placed her glass on the table beside her and lifted her feet to rest on the coffee table.

"It's been so long since I dreamed it." She shook her head in an attempt to dispel the sense of panic surging inside her. "Just when I think I've got everything under control, it comes back to remind me."

She sighed, and was suddenly grateful for the boy's inadvertent intervention. At least she'd been spared those awful minutes between nightmare and waking, when she couldn't tell the difference between the two. Today it had been mere seconds of confusion. Fire. Explosion. Death. It never changed, not a single detail. And she always awoke with a scream.

"I refuse to think about it." She shoved her glasses onto her face and tried to focus on the pages in her lap. It took a while, though. The tears that welled in her eyes wouldn't go away until she could turn her mind from the horror of the past, and she couldn't do that until she concentrated on something else.

But her will to survive was strong. Eventually, she began to make sense of the words on the page. The moment of horror had passed, and her pencil made odd-looking tracks across the typed page, changing a word here, a comma there.

It was over.

It had been over five years ago.

Hank Alton braked the four-wheel-drive truck to a smooth stop and shut off the motor. Getting out, he thrust his hands into his trouser pockets and took stock of the scene of yesterday's crime.

He'd never been out this way before, to the house at the end of Blossom Lane.

He wasn't exactly thrilled to be there now. He hadn't had much choice, though. Willie owed Mad Sally an apology for trying to steal her apples. Hank hadn't wanted him to come alone, however, so he'd arranged to meet Willie there after football practice.

A brief glance at his watch assured him he was a few minutes early, so he took a moment to study the place. The house was surprisingly pleasing to the eye, redwood and old stone with large windows to make it seem light and airy, even from the outside. It didn't look anything like a witch's den. Even the garden belied that image, the thick carpet of grass bordered by masses of flowers.

It looked like a perfectly normal home. But then, he hadn't expected anything else, he told himself. It wasn't as though he really believed everything he'd heard about Mad Sally. Not even Willie's dramatic recounting of his near-capture had swayed Hank's conviction that the woman in residence was not a witch.

He wasn't convinced, though, that she wasn't just a tad loony. There was certainly enough evidence to support that theory. In the two years since he and his family had come to live in Oakville, he'd heard the strange tales of the madwoman who lived at the end of Blossom Lane. She dressed in a hooded robe, wailed at intruders, and talked to rocks and flowers.

That last tidbit had come from a child who had been hiding behind the stone wall when Mad Sally walked past, talking a blue streak. The child had sworn there was no one else there to listen. She said odd stuff like, "It's a lovely day for growing, don't you think?" and "I've got work to do this morning, but I'll be out this afternoon to keep you company." Odd— not in content but in context. Did she think the rocks and flowers cared?

Frankly, Hank thought the child had been exaggerating. But Willie's fear had been real, and it had almost been against Hank's better judgment to encourage his son's decision to apologize. But fears aside, Willie was eleven now, old enough to make his own choices about the kind of person he wanted to be. Hank's heart swelled with pride as he remembered his conversation with the boy.

"What do you suppose you ought to do about this?" he'd asked his son across the dinner table, after hearing the sensational details of that afternoon's escapade, including a description of Mad Sally that set new standards for the word "ugly."

Willie had sighed as though he knew the answer but didn't want to say it aloud. Hank had had to wait, but not for long.

"I think I need to apologize."

"Why?"

"Because it was wrong of me to try to steal the apples."

"You didn't get away with any?"

Willie shook his head. "I ran when she turned her back."

Hank nodded solemnly. "Understandable." He let a minute or so pass, idly watching as Catherine, his mother, puttered at the other end of the country kitchen, putting to rights the aftermath of their dinner. Then he asked about Willie's fall. "I still can't figure that part out," Hank said. "You haven't taken a tumble like that in years. Did a branch break?"

Willie's eyes rounded as he relived the moment of

terror. "It was a scream, Dad. Just like something out of a horror movie! Scared me half to death."

A scream? Hank wondered, and shook his head. He really didn't have a clue what went on in that house at the end of Blossom Lane. He wasn't sure he wanted to find out.

"Why do you suppose she won't let us have the crab apples?" Willie asked. "Everyone knows they're too sour to eat."

"It doesn't matter, Son. It's her tree."

"It's her tree," Hank repeated to himself, and focused on the infamous ammunition dump. He couldn't help but grin, because the tree was literally brimming with apples—a definite temptation regardless of the hazards! Somehow, he found it hard to believe a missing apple or two would cause so much grief.

His gaze flickered across the No Trespassing signs posted at intervals along the stone wall. For whatever reason, Mad Sally was determined to protect that which was hers.

He checked his watch again. His son was running late. On the very remote chance that Willie had already taken the initiative, Hank let himself into the garden and strode up the sidewalk to the front door. He knocked, waited a few moments, then knocked again. There was no answer. Evidently, Mad Sally wasn't home.

He was about to turn away when his eyes caught a flash of movement. He peered through the glass of the front door and saw it again, a swirl of purple at the end of a darkened hallway. There was definitely someone in the house. He pounded on the door, more forcefully this time. No one came.

He decided to go around back. As he rounded the corner to the side of the house, he found himself confronted by a series of long, angular hedges that were cut about knee height. He stepped across the top of one and followed a grassy path in the same general direction he wished to go. He had to cross over the tops of three more before he reached the far side. Looking back, he realized he'd just negotiated a tiny maze.

He'd also cheated.

Hank knew he was grinning when he walked around the last corner and could clearly see a woman through the wide expanse of windows at the back of the house. He stopped in a shadow for a moment to watch her.

She was standing with her back to him, stirring something in an enormous black pot on the stove. Through the billowing steam, he could make out strings of garlic and dried plants of some sort tied up and hung above the stove. Fragments of fairy tales assaulted him, and for a brief moment he wondered if everything he'd heard about her was true.

But then she turned, and Hank discovered one thing no one had ever hinted.

She was lovely. He made a mental note to get Willie's eyes checked as his gaze drifted over her.

Rich brown hair fell heavily to her shoulders with only a hint of curl at the bottom. There were streaks of lighter colors through it, he noticed, and he would have said they were from the sun if it weren't for the almost porcelain tone of her skin. Thick dark eyebrows slanted over eyes that were the lightest blue he'd ever seen. The contrast was startling, almost mesmerizing. Her features were strong, forgoing delicacy in favor of good lines and well-proportioned bone structure. Her cheekbones were high, her lips full, her chin softly rounded, her nose straight and not at all pointed. Hank looked hard but couldn't find a single wart.

She didn't look like a witch.

She hadn't seen him yet, and he watched as she rose up on her toes to delve into a cabinet above the sink. Shutting it, she moved on to another. Her wine-colored skirt whirled from hip to calf, giving him a tantalizing glimpse of shapely legs before his gaze was drawn higher. A sleeveless knit shirt of the same color clung to her body, and he could easily see the generous swell of her breasts as she reached high above. He enjoyed the view.

He continued watching her, somehow reluctant to tear his gaze from the swinging rhythm of her hips as she moved around the kitchen. She wasn't overly tall, but she wasn't a tiny person either. Big enough to scare little children, though. And bigger children. Like Willie. Hank remembered his reason for being there just as she turned away and went back to stirring whatever it was on the stove. He left the shadow and mounted the three concrete steps that led to the kitchen door. He knocked.

She kept on stirring.

He knocked louder.

She ignored him.

If she was a witch, she was certainly a rude one. Hank wasn't used to being ignored. He tried the door knob and found that it turned easily. Opening the door slightly, he knocked again. She gave no sign that she knew he was there. He could hear her humming, a discordant melody that would have hurt his ears if it had been any louder.

Mad Sally was beginning to get on his nerves. Hank considered leaving well enough alone, but he couldn't. Something that had absolutely nothing to do with Willie made him want to stay.

And there was always the chance that his son was somewhere inside. He didn't really think so. Willie might be daring enough to brave the apple tree, but Hank was fairly certain his nerve wouldn't hold up to facing Mad Sally on his own.

Still, he had to know for sure.

Taking a deep breath, he thrust open the door and crossed the kitchen to tap her on the shoulder.

She screamed, a harsh, shrill noise that blanketed the air. He covered his ears in self-defense, suddenly understanding why Willie had fallen out of the tree. Her scream was formidable.

Then he looked into her eyes and realized she was terrified. The last thing he'd expected was for her to be afraid, and he didn't want that. He backed away, fast. She lost her defensive posture as he retreated, and he was almost pleased when she grabbed the spoon from the pot and began to wave it aggressively at him. She was better now.

Then he saw gobs of red stuff drip off the spoon and hit the floor with a hiss. He half expected the linoleum to curdle.

"I didn't mean to scare you," he said softly, when he'd backed right up against the door, "but you didn't answer when I knocked." She cocked her head and looked at him as though he'd stepped off a spaceship. Hank wasn't encouraged.

He tried again, using the calming tone he used with clients who were on the verge of panic. "I'm Hank Alton. My son was supposed to meet me here." He waited for another long moment, during which he could hear the red stuff bubbling on the stove.

"Who are you?"

Her voice was an agreeable surprise—low and husky, the complete opposite of her earlier shriek. It matched her lips, he thought idly, and knew precisely why that assessment pleased him. He very much liked the shape of her mouth, the sound of her voice. It was a physical gratification that strummed his masculine responses.

Then what she had said sank in. *Who are you?* Hell! He'd already answered that question! He hid his irritation and said his name again, hoping that this time she'd pay attention. "Hank Alton."

"Hancock?" Her brows knit together, and she slowly lowered the spoon. "You mean you scared me half to death just to sell me *insurance*?"

He looked at her in disbelief. "Not Hancock. Hank

Alton," he said, speaking very slowly and with firm emphasis on each syllable. "I've come about Willie."

"A will? Since when do insurance companies care if you have a will? Is this some sort of threat?" She raised the spoon again.

Hank gritted his teeth against the temptation to shout. This was tougher than he'd imagined. He kept his voice soft, though, when he tried again. She was jumpy enough already. No telling what she could do with that spoon if she had a mind to. "Not a will. *Willie.* My son. He was supposed to meet me here."

Her expression turned threatening, her clear blue eyes throwing out warning flashes. "There's a rumor going around that I shoot trespassers."

He forgot about not yelling. *"You shot Willie?"*

It was the first thing to come out of his mouth that Sally understood. She stared at the nearly apoplectic man across the room and decided he was much too concerned about this Willie to do her any harm. Amazing what a little threat could do.

"You shot my son?"

His son. No wonder he was screaming.

"No need to get excited," she said calmly. "Of course I didn't shoot anyone."

His expression of relief had a quality of frustration in it that she recognized. It wasn't easy carrying on a conversation without her hearing aids. She was about to explain when she noticed the blobs of red on the floor. "Rats! Now look what's happened!"

She grabbed a wet cloth from the sink and knelt down, then remembered there was much more of the stuff still cooking away on the stove.

"Oh, no! The pot!" She bounced back up to check on the extent of damage. Burying her face in the steam, she sniffed. "Doesn't smell burned," she said cautiously. "Maybe there's hope." She stuck in her spoon and was just beginning to stir when the gong sounded.

Another interruption! Blast it all anyway, she

thought. She'd gone five years without having so much as a single visitor inside her home, and now she had one in the kitchen and another waiting at the front door.

"Oh, what to do? What to do?" she muttered, whirling to face the intruder at the other end of the kitchen. He looked paralyzed, staring at her with an expression that bespoke his total lack of comprehension of the noise that still reverberated throughout the house. Sally couldn't blame him. The gong was pretty offensive if you weren't used to it.

He didn't mean to harm her, she realized. He'd already passed on that opportunity. Besides, he wasn't dressed for the job. The colorful silk tie that was obviously designer-styled, Italian loafers, and tailor-made suit were not apropos to any physically threatening crime scenario she could imagine.

No, he didn't mean to harm her. Harmless, however, was not how she would describe him.

Distinguished? Absolutely—particularly with all that lovely graying hair that he wore just a smidgen longer than might be called conservative.

Interesting? Decidedly. A hint of raw sensuality was not quite hidden beneath the veneer of sophisticated male. She almost laughed aloud, surprised that her responses could be so attuned after five years of living like a hermit.

Handsome? Unquestionably. Dark brows slashed over gold-flecked green eyes that were warmly mysterious. A weathered tan smoothed across uncompromisingly masculine features—a firm chin with the barest suggestion of a cleft, a mouth that looked both soft and hard. With a feminine interest that was nearly foreign to her, she wondered which it was. Soft . . . or hard?

She caught herself just seconds from asking. "Ragged social skills, Sally," she murmured disparagingly as the gong sounded again. She decided she was going to have to trust him. It was either that or ignore the door gong, and she couldn't afford to do that because it might be the express carrier with the galleys of Sarah's book.

"You come over here and stir while I answer the door," she demanded.

"I didn't come—"

"I know you don't want to stir it," she interrupted, "but if it's ruined, it'll be your fault, because you frightened me half out of my wits, and I think you owe me at least a minute of your time for just waltzing in the door without so much as a by-your-leave." She crossed the room and waggled the spoon in his face.

She wasn't surprised when he reached out for it. He didn't look like the kind of guy who would balk at lending a hand in a pinch. But when his fingers curled around hers, she felt the shock all the way to her toes. The sensual awareness was so unexpected, it rushed past her defenses before she could even take a breath.

It was incredibly important that he not realize how completely he'd rattled her. Dragging her stunned gaze from the hands that were coupled so intimately around the spoon, she gritted her teeth and looked up at the stranger. Before she could marshal any sort of indignation—the thing she was *supposed* to feel— the large, masculine hand slid from hers to settle farther up the handle.

She stared at him for a long moment and wished she knew him well enough to judge whether or not he'd done it on purpose. If it was accidental, she thought, it was definitely hit-and-run. From his maddeningly blank expression it might not have happened at all.

The gong sounded for the third time.

Escape seemed to be a sensible endeavor. "I'll be right back," she warned, glaring up at him. "Don't forget to stir."

With a swirl of her skirt, she was gone. Hank

watched her hips undulate as she strode down the hallway, until the bubbling on the stove stole his attention. Hesitantly, remembering where he was and who *she* was, he approached the stove. He put the spoon in the pot and hoped for the best.

Two

Willie fared no better than his dad.

Sally recognized the boy the second she threw open the door. "Your bucket is by the gate," she said after a short pause, stunned that he had actually come to her door. To date, the only children who dared to ring the gong had done so at inconvenient hours, their intentions simply to disturb Mad Sally in her lair.

The dark-haired boy mumbled something she didn't catch, and she tried again to hurry him on his way. "I'm glad you weren't hurt," she said gently. "I left your bucket by the gate, and you're welcome to take it."

He gulped and said something that sounded like, "Isd wieroi apweri iedfsdffyy."

Sally smiled politely and hoped he'd take that as polite understanding. He remained glued to the stoop. She couldn't figure out why he didn't leave, except that there was a curiously befuddled look on his face that reminded her of the man in the kitchen. *That was it!* In a flash she realized they were either there on the same mission, or there was an epidemic of confused males running around Oakville.

She decided to make an exception to her rule

because she really did want to discover why the boy had knocked on her door. She invited him in.

He hesitated.

"I won't bite," she said, grinning.

He looked very reluctant to believe her.

She tried again. "If you'll come in, I'll do something about figuring out why you're here. Or you can stand there and wait. It's up to you." He didn't budge, so she shrugged and retreated, leaving the door open in case he changed his mind.

She didn't think he would. Mad Sally's reputation was really quite wicked.

"I'll just be a minute," she called over her shoulder as she crossed the living room to her bedroom. After shutting the door firmly behind her, she pulled open a drawer of the antique jewelry box that stood on her dresser and found the pair of tiny hearing aids. With an expertise that bespoke years of practice, she fitted one into each ear. Fluffing her hair back into place, she glanced in the mirror and was surprised to find herself smiling.

"Now, what on earth do you have to smile about, Sally?" she asked softly. "A man touches your hand, and you practically fall at his feet. It was an accident, for Pete sake!"

No, it wasn't, said a tiny voice in her head. He'd been hiding something behind that blank expression.

"Get a grip, Sally!" she said impatiently. "Your imagination is working overtime. There are strangers in your home, and you've got to deal with them." She wasn't exactly sure how, though. They were her first visitors in five years.

All senses functioning, she briskly walked back to the living room, only to discover the front door was closed. She was just about to despair that she'd bothered with the hearing aids for nothing, when she heard the rumble of masculine laughter in the kitchen. She followed the sound the way a moth seeks light.

It had been so long.

Their backs were to her when she entered the room, and she hesitated, trying very hard not to laugh at what they were saying.

"I thought you told me her eyes bulged," the man said, "and that her face was all smashed and wrinkled."

The boy shrugged. "Maybe she was sick."

"Or perhaps your imagination got the better of you?"

The boy shook his head. "Not even imagination is that good. Maybe she has an ugly twin."

"And maybe you fell on your head."

Sally watched as the boy took the spoon and dropped a blob of the stuff from the pot onto the counter. He blew on it energetically, then dipped his finger into the cooling mound. The finger went to his mouth. After a moment he smacked his lips. "It's jam, Dad."

"No kidding?" The man took a similar taste, and she tried very hard to smother a giggle at his next words. "How can you be sure it's not bat wings and gizzards?"

The boy shrugged. "I'll bet they don't taste this good."

"Good instincts," she said, smiling mischievously as she sauntered across the room. "And it's jelly. Crab-apple jelly. Not jam. Certainly not bat wings and gizzards. They're out of season."

They spun around and stared in identical disbelief. She giggled and couldn't resist adding the punch line. "Gizzards are too high in cholesterol." Reaching the stunned duo at the stove, she retrieved the spoon from the boy and dipped it into the pot.

"It's not burned," the man said.

She looked up to find his assessing gaze fixed on her. The amused gleam in his eyes told her he might not be as gullible as she believed. There was also a hint of something else—something very masculine that had nothing to do with jelly and gizzards.

"Thank you for stirring it." She turned back to her pot, wishing . . . She hoped the steam would hide the sudden rush of blood to her cheeks. No man had looked at her like that in so long.

She stirred the jelly. The two males shifted uncomfortably beside her.

She waited. It was for them to tell her why they were in her home.

The boy finally spoke. "I came to apologize for stealing your apples . . . for *trying* to steal your apples."

She hadn't expected that. In all the years since she'd moved to Oakville, no one had apologized for anything. A stranger infiltrating a small community, she'd sought only peace. Quiet. Privacy.

The townspeople had treated her antisocial yearnings as abnormal. She was an oddity. Eccentric, her kinder neighbors had called her in the beginning. She had used that to suit her own ends, playing the part with a dramatic flair that was surprisingly easy.

"Eccentric" soon changed to "crazy." She became Mad Sally. And because of that, no apologies were necessary. Yet this young man was apologizing.

Taking a deep breath, she carefully turned down the flame beneath the pot and turned to him. Holding his frightened yet determined gaze with her own, she smiled. "Thank you very much. I'm pleased to accept your apology." She glanced at the man who was standing just behind the boy, his large hand resting on the young man's shoulder, and suddenly divined their relationship. Her smile broadened, and her gaze flickered back to the shorter of the duo.

"You must be Willie."

"How did you know?" the man asked.

"I may be mad," she said softly, looking at him, "but I'm not stupid. He has your eyes." She smiled again.

"Besides, I think you yelled something about him earlier."

"You yelled at her?" asked Willie, tilting his head to stare at his father.

Hank glanced at his son and shrugged. "Seemed to be the thing to do." When he looked back at Sally, though, his expression held none of the frustration she'd noticed when he'd first entered her kitchen.

She was intrigued. Why had they come, when no one had ever bothered with Mad Sally? A little theft of apples, that was all.

Yet here they were. It warmed her heart, a sensation she'd not felt in so long, it almost brought tears to her eyes. She was tempted by that warming, so very tempted. And he was looking at her as though it was conceivable she was a normal person, one he wouldn't mind getting to know. But, as she'd just pointed out, she wasn't stupid.

Friends were dangerous. Lovers, worse. They led to heartbreak.

Married lovers were unthinkable. And that's exactly what he was. Married. Father and son meant there had to be a mother, a wife, in the background.

Stiffening her back and her resolve as she remembered who she was and how she'd managed to survive thus far, she turned back to the giant pot of jelly. "Willie, I appreciate your apology and sincerely hope you'll ask your friends not to steal apples from my garden again. I have a use for them, one that is more essential than throwing them about the fields."

"Yes, ma'am."

She almost smiled at that. "Your mother and father have raised a very polite son," she said without thinking. "They should be proud."

"I don't have a mother." The plainly spoken words tugged at heartstrings she'd thought were locked away. Shocked by her reaction, she barely stopped herself from telling Willie that he was a very lucky boy to have even one parent. She'd been raised without either.

She'd also been raised not to pry. This little chit-chat had gone on long enough, she decided.

She filled her lungs with the steamy scent of crab apples. "I need to finish putting this up now. Please go."

She felt their hesitation and froze, afraid they'd want more from her.

She had nothing to give.

Hank stared at the back of her head. It was on the tip of his tongue to say no, that he wasn't ready to leave yet. He wanted to stay. He wanted to make her smile again, because her warmth had touched him.

He wanted to know why she acted crazy as a loon one minute and serenely sane the next. He caught himself before he put the thoughts into words. Wrong place. Wrong time. Wrong woman.

Willie shifted nervously under his hand. Hank squeezed his son's shoulder in reassurance. In silence they left her standing over the steaming pot as they retreated across the linoleum to the back door. Hank gently pulled it closed. As he followed Willie around the side of the house and through the maze, he thought about his unexpected response to the woman inside the house.

He wondered if he was crazy to want to know Mad Sally.

She should have felt relief when she heard their footsteps cross the kitchen floor. She didn't.

She heard the door click shut, and only then did she wonder if she'd sacrificed too much for peace of mind.

Too much for sanity.

Long into the night Sally wondered if she'd sacrificed her heart . . . even though she'd sought to save it from dying of sadness.

Hank strode out of the Fairview courthouse and shook hands with his client one last time. It had been a hard-fought battle, but after a week of securing testimony from witnesses and presenting physical evidence, he'd convinced the court that his client was innocent. The charge had been arson, setting fire to his expensive home for the insurance. Hank had known he was innocent, but proving it had been an incredible challenge.

He clapped his client on the shoulder and they parted, Hank heading for his truck. His stomach rumbled as he pulled out of the lot, and he debated the merits of driving the thirty miles back to Oakville for a late lunch at home versus stopping in Fairview. Pushing a pair of buttons, he lowered the windows to let the summer breeze inside. A second rumbling made up his mind. Fairview it was.

He turned right at the corner, heading toward a small diner he frequented on his trips to Fairview. Stopping at a red light, he idly drummed his fingers on the steering wheel, not in a great hurry to go anywhere. He was considering the pros and cons of taking the rest of the afternoon off when he noticed a woman exiting a shop on the corner across the street. She wore a bright yellow dress that nipped in at the waist and flared over slender hips. High-heeled sandals made the glimpses of her calves rewarding as she walked down the street in the opposite direction. Hank was just thinking that there was something familiar about the delightful swing of her hips, when she opened the door of a blue sports car and turned to put something behind the driver's seat.

Mad Sally was loose in Fairview.

Hank didn't know which surprised him more— seeing her there or discovering that she drove a flashy sports car. He was wondering where she'd left her trademark hooded cloak when the car behind him honked. Without making a conscious decision, he steered his truck across the intersection and pulled over to the curb.

Three cars were parked between them, but thanks to the height of the truck, Hank was afforded a clear picture of the woman in yellow. He watched as she slammed her car door shut without getting inside, then stared after her as she jaywalked across the street and slipped inside a store. He killed the truck's engine and waited.

It was a hardware store, he mused. What could she need there that she couldn't find in Oakville? Then he remembered something Willie had told him. Mad Sally didn't shop in Oakville. Not even for groceries. She was rarely ever seen away from the cottage at the end of Blossom Lane, and only then be-robed and be-deviling, or so it was said.

Hank had never once heard a whisper of a yellow dress or a blue sports car.

Ten minutes later he'd almost convinced himself that it was a case of mistaken identity, when the woman in yellow left the store. He strained his eyes as he watched her stroll down the street in his direction, tucking a package under her arm. Her hair swung lightly at her shoulders as she turned every now and then to peer at various shop windows. She was almost directly across the street from him when she disappeared inside another store.

There was no doubt in his mind at all. Hank rested his elbow on the open window and settled down to wait for Mad Sally to reappear.

This time it was only five minutes before she was back on the sidewalk. Another package dangled from her wrist as she stepped into the street and made a diagonal crossing toward her car. He winced as she skipped between slowly moving cars, but somehow he wasn't much surprised that she'd overlooked the safety of the crosswalk just a few feet away. Doing the safe thing evidently wasn't her style.

He watched as she slipped into the car and pulled the door shut. Turning the key in the truck's ignition, he waited until the blue car left the curb before following. She didn't drive very fast, and he was hard-pressed to stay off her bumper as she led him around the block and back toward the center of town. He concentrated on driving because he didn't want to examine too closely what he was doing.

Following this woman was definitely in the "questionable" category. Even so, he didn't have the slightest inclination to stop. Mad Sally's portrayal of a perfectly normal woman performing perfectly ordinary errands fascinated him no end.

Several blocks later the blue car slipped into an empty parking spot. Hank swore as he looked for a suitable place for his own truck. There wasn't anything in sight, and with midtown traffic at the height of its noon rush, double-parking was out of the question. Rounding the corner, he sped around the block. He returned just in time to see her slide back into her car.

His stomach rumbled as he waited for her to get in front of him. He was thinking about lunch again when he noticed a short, balding man with a large carton in his arms dash out of a bank just a few feet from where the blue car was parked. He heard him call out "Sally" at the same moment that she pulled into traffic and sped off down the street.

His curiosity piqued, Hank didn't think twice about stopping. He quickly slipped into the spot Sally had just vacated, threw the gearshift into park, and ran around the hood of the truck. He caught up with the man at the bank's door. "You wanted to catch Ma—er, Sally?" he asked, thinking at the last second that perhaps "Mad Sally" wasn't the appropriate thing to call her.

The man with the carton looked at him suspiciously for a moment. "You know Sally?"

Hank nodded. "I'm from Oakville," he said, hoping that would be enough of a tie. It was the best he could offer.

Apparently it was good enough, because the man smiled. Juggling the carton under one arm, he offered his hand. "I'm Morton Campbell. I manage the bank here."

"Hank Alton. I was driving by when I saw you chasing after Sally. Anything I can do?" This was a fine line he was crossing, Hank realized. His curiosity against her privacy. He thought he was justified, if only to satisfy his compelling urge to discover the real woman behind the myth. The woman he'd watched for the last few minutes wasn't anything like the recluse about whom bizarre tales were told. He had witnessed an unremarkable outing in the life of a sane, rational woman. Even the jaywalking wasn't extraordinary. Foolish behavior, perhaps, but not particularly aberrant.

Campbell grinned and handed him the box. "Sally left these empty jars when she dropped off the jelly. With that tree of hers dropping fruit as fast as she can pick it up, she'll need them."

Hank had no choice but to take it. "Jelly?" he asked, remembering the steaming black pot on Sally's stove. "Crab-apple jelly?"

Campbell nodded. "She makes it for a soup kitchen in Denver. My wife and I volunteer there a couple times a month, so we sometimes carry the jelly up and bring back the empty jars when Sally can't make it herself." He took out a large plaid handkerchief and mopped a few beads of sweat from his bald pate. "Too bad about that trip to New York next week. She'll really have to scramble to keep up with all those apples."

Hank had a sudden mental picture of Mad Sally bustling up Fifth Avenue in her cloak and decided Campbell must be mistaken about New York. Swallowing hard over his laugh, he said, "I wasn't aware Sally volunteered at a soup kitchen. How long has she been doing it?"

"Oh, three or four years now, I expect. I think she got the idea from Maude Stemple over at the library."

"The library?"

"Mmm. Maude is always cornering people about volunteering, and I guess she must have caught Sally when she was over there." Campbell smiled his approval. "I was glad to have Sally join up. She's a real good worker."

Hank nodded as though he knew her well enough to agree. "I agree, Mr. Campbell—"

"Call me Mort," the other man interrupted, stuffing the handkerchief back into his trouser pocket. "Sally does."

Sally did a lot of things Hank was having trouble believing. "As I was saying, Mort, Sally certainly keeps busy. Hard to believe she has time for all those eccentricities—"

"What eccentricities?" Mort's eyes narrowed, and Hank thought he looked as if he were about to suggest he revert to calling him Mr. Campbell. "Sally's not eccentric," Mort stated flatly.

"You don't think it's odd that she lives in Oakville and does all her shopping here in Fairview?" Hank asked.

"Oh, that." Mort looked relieved. "Sally told me that her parents once lived in Fairview a long time ago. Seems it feels more like home to her. That's why she comes over to shop and things."

"So why doesn't she live here?"

"Says she couldn't find a place she liked. Besides, we don't really see her all that often. Couple times a month, give or take." Mort put out his hand, and Hank had to shift the box to shake it. "Wish she'd find a place and move here, though. This town could use a few more good people like her." He thanked Hank again for taking the jars and pulled open the door to the bank.

Mort was half inside when he paused and looked back. "Now that you mention it, though, there is something a mite odd about that girl."

"What?" This was more like it, Hank thought. He waited as the older man took his time picking out the words.

"Well, every time she goes out of town, she brings her pet over to board here at the kennel."

"What's so odd about that?" Hank asked, a little disappointed. He didn't see anything strange about that at all, outside of the fact that there was a perfectly good kennel in Oakville. But coming to Fairview was all part of the pattern for Mad Sally. "Lots of people take their cats and dogs to kennels."

"It's a rabbit." Mort shook his head in total bewilderment. "A big white rabbit. She doesn't even keep it outside like you'd think, but treats it like a house pet. Now cats, dogs—those I understand. Never heard of someone keeping a rabbit inside, though. Kind of odd, if you ask me. Eccentric, if you want to call it that." He shrugged and disappeared inside the bank.

Hank was left on the sidewalk with more questions and only one person left to ask. Staring down at the box in his hands, he knew he was looking at his excuse to pay a return visit to the house at the end of Blossom Lane.

Sally zipped along the narrow country road that wound around the back side of Oakville. She had the road to herself, not surprisingly. She rarely met anyone on this road, which was precisely why she used it. Not that she would be recognized if someone happened to pass.

The Mad Sally everyone knew and feared was an anonymous figure hidden within the shadowy folds of her cloak. She certainly wasn't the young brunette behind the wheel of a snappy sports car.

Sally grinned. The deception she'd worked so hard to perfect had, over the years, become something of a game. The challenge of maintaining a hermit's existence on the fringes of civilization had slowly evolved from necessity to entertainment.

Five years ago, though, it had been her only means of survival.

She had fled across the country from New England to the unknown vastness of Colorado for one reason. Privacy. She neither wanted nor needed anyone to know, to care about . . . and, perhaps, to love.

Loving someone could rip your heart in two. She had survived that event once, but just barely. She didn't intend to allow it to happen again.

Extreme pain had called for extreme measures. At first she'd merely sought to cut herself off from people, to lead the life of a recluse. The fluke that had created Mad Sally had been an opportunity she'd seized with full understanding of what she was doing. Mad Sally gave her the one thing she wanted, the privacy her heart craved.

Mad Sally kept the world at bay.

To sustain that distance, she totally avoided shopping in Oakville in favor of Fairview. It was easier to keep even casual acquaintances at an emotional distance when she only saw them once or twice a month.

People like Willie and his father were capable of changing everything.

What would they say, she wondered, when they told their friends about their encounter with Mad Sally? Would they say she walked, talked, and breathed like a human being—and not a witch? Would they plant seeds of suspicion that would lead people to doubt that Sally was truly mad?

Would they get curious enough to want to discover the truth? What really bothered her was that she didn't particularly mind if they did.

"Would it be so bad," she asked herself, "to have the postman say hello instead of leaving everything in the box and beating a fast retreat?" She spoke aloud, as though the proximity to her home somehow pressured her to get back into character. Mad Sally always talked to herself.

"Why should I feel threatened if a Girl Scout wants to sell me some cookies? And if the Avon lady wants to put her little magazine on my door handle, will my life fall apart?"

She'd been asking herself these and similar questions for several days now, ever since Willie and his dad had invaded her home.

After five years of avoiding her neighbors, she was suddenly afraid she'd gone too far.

"That's a pretty big ego you've got there, Sally," she muttered. "What makes you imagine either Willie or his father gave you any second thoughts at all?"

Braking hard, she guided the car into a rutted lane, then drove another mile or so with proper attention to potholes and other hazards. She'd discovered this back entrance to her home just days after she'd bought the property. It afforded her the freedom to come and go as she pleased, without giving her neighbors even a hint of how she managed to handle the details of everyday living.

"They probably think I ride my broomstick to the market," she said, patting her more practical mode of transportation on its dashboard.

Pulling up to the garage behind her house, she punched the mechanism for the automatic door. She guided the car into the dark interior, parked, and loaded her arms with packages. The sack of groceries, block of paraffin, and hacksaw were cumbersome, but she managed to get everything inside the house without much trouble.

She left the box of pistachio nuts she'd bought for her rabbit's birthday party in the car. Tonight, after he was asleep, she'd sneak outside and wrap it.

Three

When Sally caught herself itching to make corrections to the best-seller she was reading, she threw it onto the sofa beside her. "Stupid book," she muttered, picking up the television program schedule she'd saved from the Sunday paper.

She had that problem a lot, wanting to edit books that were already in print. That frustration was just one of the things she'd learned to live with since she began earning her living as a consulting editor. She'd also had to learn to deal with anxious authors and deadlines.

She really didn't mind either of those, not as a rule. They were part of the job. Tonight, though, she didn't want to work.

She didn't know what she wanted.

"Summer reruns are not the answer, Sally girl." Tossing the TV schedule on top of the discarded book, she stood up and stretched. Her light blue knit top pulled out of her skimpy denim shorts, and she absently tucked it back in as she wandered over to the umbrella plant in the corner. She pinched off a yellow leaf and twirled it in her fingers.

"I know what you feel like," she said, addressing the leaf. "One day you're green and healthy and everything's fine. Then all of a sudden you're turning colors and wanting different things than before, a different kind of fertilizer, less water, more water. You get so confused, you can't figure out *what* it is you need."

She tossed the leaf into the wastebasket. "Look in the mirror, Sally," she said with grim amusement, "and keep saying 'I'm not a leaf. . . . I'm not a leaf. . . .'"

She clasped her arms with her hands and literally took her own advice. It didn't work, though. The tension inside her was growing, and she knew it.

"I didn't have this problem last week," she complained, flicking off the overhead lights. The room was plunged into darkness. "I was content, before he came." She stood at the window, waiting patiently as her eyes adjusted. After a few moments the crab-apple tree came into focus, its silhouette a tangle of limbs against the night sky.

It didn't occur to her to question her absorbing interest in Willie's father. She might be a recluse by choice, but there was nothing in the ground rules that said she couldn't recognize sexual awareness when it rose up and smacked her in the face. And just because this was the first time it had happened in five very long and lonely years didn't mean she'd forgotten the feeling.

One way or the other, though, it didn't really matter. There was nothing she could do about it. That particular option belonged to Willie's father. And he thought she was mad.

"I will be content again," she said softly. "He won't be back. There's no reason for him to come. Soon now, he'll fade from my mind." Lifting a hand, she pressed it lightly against the cool window. "It's what I want. To be alone, to be content."

Her words sounded empty, though. Sally swore under her breath, quietly because there were certain phrases that shouldn't be said aloud . . . not even if there was no one to hear.

Years of self-reliance made an emphatic pitch for reason. He'd probably laugh, she told herself, if he knew how she was feeling . . . what she was thinking. He had no more interest in Mad Sally than anyone else in town.

Yet whose fault was that? she asked rhetorically. She was the one who'd cut herself off from everyone. She was the one who'd wanted to be a hermit. Now she had what she wanted, so she'd better stop whining about it.

"Do something physical," she advised herself aloud. "Anything." Her gaze fell on the ground beneath the tree. It was lumpy. Fallen fruit, she presumed.

"I'm going to pick up apples," she decided in a burst of determined energy. "And then I'm going to make jelly." She trotted down the hallway to the kitchen, found her bucket, and headed outside. Slamming the front door behind her, she stalked across the lawn. "I'm going to collect apples and make jelly until I'm too tired to think. And if he's still in my mind tomorrow, I'll do it again." She moved toward one of the lumps and nearly tripped when her bare foot curled over another that she hadn't seen.

"Suppose I should get a flashlight," she muttered. Returning to the house, she rooted in a closet until she saw a pair of tiki torches stashed in the corner. She'd bought a bunch of them earlier in the summer for use as antimosquito devices.

"Just the ticket for a dark night," she said, and dashed into the kitchen for matches. Remembering the slight chill of the night, she stopped at the front door to pull on her cloak. She decided against fetching shoes out of consideration for her toes. They liked the cool grass.

It took only moments to push the torches into the ground and set them afire. Just in time, too, because the gremlins of the night—bloodthirsty mosquitoes—

were suddenly buzzing around her shoulders. Grimacing, she tugged the hood over her head for added protection and began to gather apples.

Barefoot in the grass, the cloak swirling around her legs, Sally concentrated on the task at hand and tried very hard to forget she'd ever laid eyes on the man she knew only as Willie's father.

Hank backed the truck out of his driveway and headed across town. He was only going to deliver the jars, he'd decided after an afternoon of second, third, and fourth thoughts. Then he'd leave, taking his curiosity with him, because it wasn't worth getting involved.

He would leave the carton on her front step and go back home to his family. To his mom and Willie. And the dog. His was a normal life, more or less—lacking a wife but what the hell, they were happy enough.

He wanted to talk to her.

She was crazy. He should avoid her, take his cue from everyone else in town and leave her alone.

She was lovely. Her smile, her voice, her eyes . . . She came to him in his sleep, ambushed him at his weakest moments.

She was indifferent. She'd turned her back and told him to leave. He should respect her wishes.

He wanted her to know she wasn't alone.

Hank was wondering where the button for her door gong was when he rounded the last bend. The spectacle that met his eyes was unexpected, unearthly . . . uncomfortably sinister. Beneath the flames of a pair of torches a lone figure swayed for a moment in the night's breeze, then suddenly bent to the ground. He slammed on the brakes and cut the engine, then just sat there, holding his breath as the cloaked figure slowly rose again and glided out of the beam of his headlights.

She waited, motionless. It was easy to see how

she'd got her name, Hank realized, as she played the scene to her best advantage. Backlighted by the torches, invisible within her ghostly cloak, Mad Sally boldly defied anyone to approach, her posture radiating the confidence of knowing no one would dare.

The hell he wouldn't!

The rest of Oakville could believe what they wanted, but damned if he was going to be played for a fool. If this scene was any kind of indication, she was deliberately building her reputation as a madwoman, brick by brick, one bizarre act after another.

He didn't buy it. *Come on, Sally, get off it!* he wanted to shout. *Stop this ridiculous charade and get a life . . . a real one!*

Or was this her reality . . . and the woman he'd followed in Fairview the sham?

He punched off the truck's headlights and stepped out of the truck, slamming the door shut behind him. He paused for a moment, giving her a chance to recognize his face so that she wouldn't be afraid. Not that she deserved the kindness, he thought, considering how she did her best to terrify the town.

He gave her the kindness, though, because he wanted to.

In the flickering light of the torches, he watched as a hand came out to pull the hood back. She shook the hair from her eyes and stared at him from the other side of her garden wall. Hank took a deep breath to clear out the cobwebs of rumor, then another to dispel his mounting anger.

It didn't work. She was going to get a piece of his mind.

Maybe she'd put it to good use.

He was too angry to bother with the delicate picket gate. He vaulted the low rock wall and strode furiously to where she waited. He had to give her credit for holding her ground. She didn't budge, not even when he pulled up just a breath away. She tipped her head back to compensate for their difference in height, and he found her luminous eyes full of wary surprise and something else that he hadn't expected.

Excitement.

His anger should have cooled a few degrees as another response heated, but it didn't. Instead, he was both furious and aroused, and needing relief for each. His gaze fell to her parted lips, and he found himself wanting to test their softness. Would she open her mouth to his?

Would she moan her pleasure when he thrust his tongue deep inside?

Had Mad Sally bewitched him? He let out a low growl. Not yet, not now! he told himself. First he was going to get to the bottom of this idiotic madwoman charade . . . if that's what it was.

It had to be.

She spoke before he had a chance. "Good evening, Mr. . . . ah, Hancock. How's Willie?"

"Willie is just fine, and my name is Hank Alton, not Hancock," he said through clenched teeth. Couldn't she get anything straight?

Sally wished he would move his lips when he talked. At least that way, she'd have a chance at sorting out the words. "Are you here about that insurance you were talking about?" She hoped not, because suddenly she had a hunger for company— specifically *his* company—and she'd rather not spend their time together talking about term versus whole-life policies.

"No."

She smiled, silently thanking him for mouthing the word so carefully. "I don't think I've introduced myself, Mr. Hancock. I'm Sally Michaels."

If the light had been better, she would have sworn his face had turned a deep red. As it was, his thunderous expression puzzled her. What was putting him so out of sorts? she wondered, thinking that perhaps he should loosen his tie just in case he was having an attack of something. And why was he wearing a tie with a cardigan sweater anyway? Was that his stab at dressing casually?

Stuffy, she thought, but gorgeous all the same.

Hank was fast becoming acquainted with new levels of frustration. "I'm beginning to agree with the rest of Oakville, because either you're crazy"—he gestured brusquely toward the torches—"or this is just a game with you. What are you playing at, Sally?" he asked with deceptive softness.

She bobbed her head. "Lovely evening, isn't it?"

"I didn't come to discuss the weather!" Dammit, he thought, didn't she know when enough was enough? He watched her gaze follow the length of his necktie, then slide across the cashmere sweater he'd pulled on in place of the suit jacket that went with his trousers. There was a hint of mischief in her eyes when she looked back at his face, but she didn't say what she was obviously thinking.

Good thing too! Hank wasn't in the mood to defend his choice of clothes, not to a woman who favored hooded cloaks and bare feet. The sweater he wore was suddenly too warm as he wondered what else was bare beneath her heavy cloak.

"It's a bit chilly out here, don't you think?" Sally asked, following his gaze downward. She debated whether or not to invite him inside and decided against it, old habits being hard to break and all that.

Looking up again, she found her gaze suddenly captured by his, and she realized he was roaring mad. She'd just decided to make a hearing-aid run when he said something else she didn't understand. Impulsively, she touched her finger to his lips, stilling the soundless words so that he could hear her own. "Hold that thought. I'll be right back." With a swirl of the heavy cloak she barefooted it back to the house and hurried inside.

She had no idea if he'd be there when she returned. She raced to her bedroom and hoped he'd be curious enough to wait.

She wanted to get to know Willie's father. Her breath caught in her throat as she wondered how she could even consider doing something so totally at odds with the lifestyle she'd designed for herself.

Then she realized she'd already made the decision to do it. She wouldn't be in there getting the hearing aids if she didn't want to know him.

She wanted to be his friend. She couldn't help herself.

She wanted him to know her, Sally Michaels. The trick now, she thought, was to figure out how to do that without the influence of Mad Sally making a muddle of everything. It wasn't as if she could just say, "I'm really not mad, you know," and expect him to believe it.

Would she even get the chance to try?

Long after it had slammed shut, Hank stared at her front door.

She'd touched his lips.

She'd asked him to wait.

She hadn't acknowledged a single thing he'd said.

He shook his head, wishing he could make some sense out of Oakville's resident enigma.

She was mad, some said—but he didn't really think so.

She was a witch, others believed. Hank seriously doubted it, although she gave a good impression of one, dancing around in that hooded cloak beneath the torches.

She was unspeakably ugly. Everyone claimed that as fact, never having seen beneath the hooded cloak. He *knew* better!

Still, glancing at the tiki torches, he could almost believe he'd imagined the episode in Fairview.

He'd give her one more chance, he decided. Then he'd go away, leaving her to her apples and mystic rites and whatever else that pleased her.

He so very much wanted to please her himself.

He looked up as the front door swung open. She

blew out in its wake, her hands at one ear as though she was . . . Well, he couldn't figure out what the hell she was doing. So he asked her, even though he realized the futility of expecting a rational answer.

"It won't go in right," she said. "Give me a sec. It'll go in if I take my time."

He understood, finally. The anger washed out of him as he contemplated the unexpected. It explained so much. "I can't believe I didn't figure it out before."

She glanced up at him with wry humor. "These things are such a nuisance when you're in a hurry." The "thing" finally settled itself comfortably in her ear, and she patted her hair back in place. "Sorry to keep you waiting, but you might have noticed that I'm pretty hopeless without my hearing aids."

"You have two?"

She nodded. "Both ears. I can't hear squat without them."

"No kidding," he said dryly. "But you do hear some things."

"The odd scream," she said, smiling broadly. "And if I'm paying attention and you raise your voice a little—"

"Or yell," he suggested.

"That usually gets through," she admitted. "I'm only partially deaf."

"Were you born that way?" Tenderness was yet another emotion he hadn't expected to feel that night, and it confused him. Just like the anger he'd experienced at her seemingly deliberate cultivation of her reputation, tenderness was a shock. There was no foundation for these emotions, no excuse.

Desire, on the other hand, needed no excuse. She was a woman he found very attractive . . . and he wanted her.

"No, I wasn't born deaf." Sally took a deep breath. She didn't want to talk about it anymore. Not tonight, the first time she'd spoken with a man who wasn't her mailman or grocer or someone associated with work. "Was there something in particular that made you drive out here, Mr. Hancock?"

He sighed. "Alton. My name is Hank Alton."

"Oh!" And how many times do you think he's told you that? she asked herself with disgust. Oh, well. In for a penny . . . "I'll bet that means you don't have anything to do with insurance."

He nodded. "I'm an attorney."

An attorney. She should have guessed. Hank Alton didn't look like a man who would be satisfied making a living selling insurance policies door to door.

"Have you already told me why you're here, Mr. Alton?" she asked, biting her lip nervously. She was beginning to realize what a fool he must think her.

"Hank," he said, and waited until she said it, too, before telling her he hadn't got around to explaining his visit. Her relief was sufficient to resurrect her smile.

"I brought your jars," he said. He backtracked to his truck and retrieved them, returning via the gate this time.

It was her turn to look confused.

"I ran into Mort Campbell this afternoon, right after you left," he said, gauging her reaction as he left out the fact that he'd never met Campbell until that day. "He tried to catch you, but I guess you didn't hear him."

She didn't say anything. She looked stunned.

"He said you make jelly for a soup kitchen up in Denver." Hank wondered if she would deny it. She didn't.

"What else did Mort tell you?" she asked, her eyes bright and clear in the glow of the torches. He held her gaze, almost mesmerized by its intensity. He could understand how that odd brightness might be construed as ghostly or frightening—especially if that was what you were expecting.

"What is there to tell?" he asked softly. "Mort just asked if I'd bring these by . . . save you a trip."

It was on the tip of her tongue to ask what he'd told Mort, but she couldn't bring herself to do it. It wasn't important. What mattered was that this man, this Hank Alton, had discovered her other side. Her alter ego. She could see it in his eyes.

But which one did he think was the real Sally Michaels? Did he even care? She avoided looking for the answer and took the carton from him. "Thank you for bringing these," she said. "I guess I'm a little surprised you'd go out of your way. You don't even know me."

"You were kind to Willie when he fell out of your tree," he said gruffly.

She set the carton on the ground and forced herself to smile up at him. Hank Alton was merely returning a favor. He hadn't come because he wanted to see her, and she shouldn't have expected that he would.

"Somehow," she said, pushing back the waves of disappointment, "I don't think Willie remembers me kindly. I frightened him half to death, and you know it."

"I think he's gotten over it." Hank smiled back at her. "The incident made him quite a hero, you know."

"A hero? For falling out of a tree?"

He shook his head. "Some of his buddies were watching from the woods across the road. They saw you come out and bend over him. From all accounts, he's the first kid to get that close to Mad Sally . . . and live to tell about it." He used her nickname purposely, to see how she'd react to it.

She laughed and rolled her eyes. "My reputation is worse than I imagined. I'm beginning to feel like the wicked witch in *Hansel and Gretel*."

"From all accounts, you haven't done anything to contradict that impression," he said, suddenly remembering the torchlighted garden. "In fact, I'd say you go out of your way to make things worse."

She looked from the torches to his suddenly stern

face in confusion. "I was picking up apples. What's wrong with that?"

"By the light of torches?"

"Tiki torches," she said. "They work better than a flashlight. And they scare away at least a portion of the mosquitoes."

It sounded too logical to be true. "Must you do it in that?" he asked, pointing to the cloak that hung shapelessly from her shoulders.

"It's chilly out here," she said simply. "I haven't changed from this afternoon when it was so hot. The cloak was the path of least resistance."

She flicked open the cloak—much like a flasher in a raincoat, he thought irrelevantly. His heart thudded in his chest as his gaze slid up over long, bare legs, impossibly brief shorts that molded tightly over slender hips, and a top that clung to the curves of her breasts. Then the giant cloak drifted shut again. His gaze shot to her face, where he expected to find the teasing half-smile of a woman who knows she's done something erotically suggestive.

She wasn't smiling at all. She was looking over the tiki-torch scene once more. When she met his eyes, her expression was totally clean of even a hint of sensual provocation. "And before you ask," she added, "the hood keeps out the mosquitoes the torches miss."

Hank was so put out with her, he barely heard the explanation. Could she be completely oblivious to the sensual vibrations he felt so strongly? Was she blind to his masculine reactions to her naked limbs and tantalizing attire? How could she be thoroughly unaffected when his body was raging with needs and desires more urgent than any he could remember?

Hank couldn't have been more wrong.

He wasn't just returning a favor, Sally realized as she stared at him. He wanted to be there. He wanted *her*—and it wasn't just a casual thought. The flames of the tiki torches were nothing compared to the desire that blazed in his eyes. She felt totally inadequate to deal with such overpowering need. Her earlier whim was suddenly unthinkable, and in a split second she changed her mind about wanting to get to know Hank Alton.

Risks like that simply weren't worth the pain.

It took an almost superhuman effort to hide her arousal from him. It was one thing to acknowledge her own sexual responses to him—stale though those might be. It was quite another to discover that the things she felt were mere twinges compared to the masculine hunger she sensed in Hank.

She wasn't equipped to handle it, to handle him. It would be like playing with fire.

Fire burned.

She concentrated on switching her thoughts to crab-apple jelly or jam or anything but the starkly sensual gleam in his eyes. Her gaze swept the torch-lighted garden, and she seized upon it.

"What did you *think* I was doing out here?" she asked, hugging herself inside the cloak.

"Something sacrificially oriented," he muttered.

She enjoyed a short laugh at his expense, almost physically moving away as she drew on Mad Sally to serve as a buffer.

"It's been months since I've sacrificed anything," she said. "And the moon isn't even full tonight." His eyes narrowed on her face, and she fought the impulse to retreat inside the hood. Defiantly, she met his gaze.

"You enjoy it, don't you?" he asked finally.

"What?"

"Your reputation. Mad Sally and all that."

"It's who I am," she said simply.

He nodded, then let his gaze drift across her face one more time. At last, apparently accepting what he saw there, he nodded again. "Then I guess I'll leave you to get on with it."

"With what?"

"That's up to you," he said enigmatically. Before

she could begin to figure that one out, he spoke again. "Just one last question, Sally."

"Yes?" The hope in her heart was stupid, she told herself. He was going to leave, and it was her fault. Her decision.

"Don't you ever get lonely?"

Four

"*Yes.*"

The word was a thready whisper in the night. It coiled around Hank's heart and squeezed until every last shred of her pain was his. It caught and held him motionless in the waning light of the tiki torches as he stared down at her upturned face, at the undisguised expression of bleak acceptance on it.

It prodded his conscience even as he tried to fathom what was worse than the loneliness. There had to be something. Sally had *deliberately* chosen her solitary lifestyle. Mad Sally was merely the tool she used to maintain it.

He felt like a bastard for throwing it in her face.

"I'm sorry," he said softly. "I had no right."

Sally blinked back the tears that threatened to spill onto her cheeks. Mad Sally was supposed to cackle, not cry, she tried to reason. She didn't want Hank to feel sorry for her. She didn't need his pity. She didn't need him . . . or anyone.

That didn't stop her from wanting him. Taking a deep breath, she tried to regain control over her rampant emotions. It wasn't easy, particularly when she wanted to fling herself into his arms and let him hold her and caress her until the weakness went away.

She watched, mesmerized, as he lifted a hand toward her. A sob caught in her throat, and she had to bite her bottom lip to keep it from quivering as she felt his fingers brush her cheek. His touch was gentle, and she had no idea she was crying until she saw the evidence of her tears on his damp fingers. She met his gaze as he brought his fingers to his mouth, trembled as his tongue lapped at the salt of her tears.

She saw no pity in the eyes that held her spell-bound. In its place was understanding of the life she'd chosen to lead . . . and confusion because he couldn't possibly know why she did it. There was something else in his expression that made her heart beat in an erratic and unfamiliar rhythm.

That something else was the hot flame of desire.

There's more to this than you can handle! She swallowed hard and held his gaze.

Run while you can! She didn't move.

Face facts! Hank wants more than you can give. She moistened her lips in anticipation of his kiss.

You're getting in over your head, Sally girl. She lifted her lips to meet his.

His mouth was firm yet tender on hers. He brushed her lips with his, demanding nothing, and giving her more than she'd ever dreamed of asking. She shivered when his hands lifted to cup her face, then found herself grasping his wrists for balance.

She couldn't bring herself to slide her hands across his shoulders. That would have brought them too close. They were only kissing. That was all she could possibly allow.

He scraped his teeth across her lips, tantalizing her with tiny bites that shot a heated comet low into her stomach. She moaned and opened her mouth to his tongue that was both curious and demanding. He explored, teased, and dared.

She cried out her disappointment when his tongue

withdrew, until she realized she was meant to follow.

Strong, masculine fingers threaded into her hair and massaged her scalp. She dug her fingernails into his wrists and stole her next breath from his mouth.

She absorbed his desire and fed it with her own. Her mouth slanted under his to give him more. His low growl of approval sent ripples of pleasure through her body.

His palms slid down her face to her neck, his fingers lightly flicking past the sensitive skin behind her ears before dipping lower. He pried her fingers from his wrists and settled her hands upon his shoulders. Sally barely noticed. She hardly realized when her fingers began to rove and explore the rippling strength she found there. Caught up in a fever that began and ended with Hank's skilled love-making, she could almost feel her blood heat and pulse with his every touch.

The cool night breeze was a welcome relief as he flipped the cloak back across her shoulders. Then his hands were there to warm her, sliding from waist to hip and gently massaging the bare skin between her shorts and top. When his fingers tightened around her hips and he pulled her into his body, she felt him against her belly. His mouth swallowed her cry of awareness, and his tongue thrust past his lips in erotic allusion to a more intimate rhythm.

Holding her hard against his thighs with one hand, he trailed the fingertips of the other hand up her spine. They circled around front until they lightly brushed the tips of her breasts, which were already hard beneath the light cotton top. She wanted more. She wanted there to be nothing between them, for his hands to claim bare skin, for his fingers to caress her aching nipples.

She wanted to rub her breasts against his naked chest.

That astonishingly graphic image was more effective than a bucket of cold water. Tearing her mouth from his. Sally pushed frantically against his shoulders. He released her, and backed away until she'd put several feet of sanity between them. Huddling in the dark shadows of the cottage, she stifled her cries of confusion behind her hand. What on earth had got into her? she asked herself. It was supposed to have been just a kiss, nothing more. A little comfort in the night.

But kissing Hank hadn't been enough!

She stared at a nearly extinguished tiki torch and dragged the edges of her cloak down from her shoulders, cowering beneath its folds as she alternately berated herself and demanded explanations. But she knew what had happened, just as she knew it had been her own fault. She'd wanted him to kiss her, had encouraged every move he'd made.

She'd also known enough to stop.

But I want more! She stifled the impulse that would have her throwing herself back into his arms, because she couldn't afford to take the chance.

By the time she had the nerve to look at Hank, he'd turned his back to her. He was facing the tree, his hands fisted at his sides, shoulders stiff with tension. Obviously, he was even less happy than she with her abrupt withdrawal. She took a couple of breaths, stalling for inspiration. She knew it was up to her to break the silence, and she didn't have a clue what she could say that might possibly excuse her behavior.

"I wouldn't have hurt you."

His voice was low and rough, and she recognized his regret without even looking at his face. But when he suddenly turned, she could see him clearly in the light of the rising moon. The anguish of his words was mimicked in his expression.

She rushed to set right the wrong. "I know that. I know you wouldn't have hurt me." She so very much wanted him to believe her, but he wouldn't even meet her gaze. Instead, he focused on a spot beyond her shoulder.

"But I frightened you," he said, and she saw his hands were still clenched at his side. It wasn't right for him to feel like this. She had to make him understand.

"You didn't frighten me." She'd frightened herself.

"You were trembling."

She almost smiled, because he was right about that part. She had been trembling . . . with excitement. "I haven't been kissed in a very long time," she said. "I guess my hormones need a refresher course in self-control."

"Don't make jokes. This isn't a comedy."

Enough was enough, she decided. "I know. But it's not tragic either. We kissed. We stopped." She retraced her steps until she was just inches from him.

He finally met her gaze. She made herself stand still under his scrutiny, and discovered that it wasn't all that difficult to summon a smile for his benefit.

"That was more than a kiss," he said, gently chiding her.

She swallowed and didn't answer.

"I shouldn't have touched you at all," Hank added. He hadn't meant to. She'd made it clear from the beginning that she had no room in her life for anyone. He didn't have the right to force his way in. But once he'd felt her soft lips, once he'd tasted her, he had stopped thinking about what she wanted.

"I shouldn't have let you," she said, "but I did. I wanted to have . . ."

"To have what?"

Sally shook her head. She couldn't even begin to explain. "You made me forget for a while," she said instead. "You took away the loneliness and made me feel wanted."

"If you're lonely, it's your choice." He wanted to touch her again, to give comfort. But he didn't.

She nodded solemnly. "It's my choice."

She could have explained, Sally knew, but it wouldn't have made any difference. It wouldn't change anything. Hank would still leave, because staying wasn't an option she could give him. Breaking away from the steady gaze that was in danger of stumbling upon the secrets she hid especially from herself, she bent over and picked up the carton of jelly jars.

She walked into her house without a backward glance.

Sally stared at her reflection in the bedroom mirror as she hurriedly removed her hearing aids. She knew he was going to leave. She just didn't want to hear it.

She hadn't wanted him to go away, not really. It was the safest thing to do, though.

I wanted to have just one good memory that was free and clear of hurt, she would have said had she been less cautious. *I wanted to remember what it's like to share something intimate with a man. You see, Hank, even though I was very much in love with my husband, he's dead now, and I can't allow myself to remember anything about him at all. Not even the good times.*

Hank wouldn't have understood, and she couldn't have explained. He wasn't to know that her husband, John, had died in the explosion that had damaged her hearing. Hank wouldn't realize that John had been the first person she'd ever loved.

He wouldn't understand that in loving John, she'd exposed herself to such suffocating heartache that she couldn't bear to remember him at all.

Sally *never* let herself think about the husband she'd once loved. She had schooled herself to avoid thinking about him altogether, because it always led to the memory of his death . . . the moment in her life when everything had gone totally, utterly wrong.

Still, she had no control over the nightmare that haunted her sleep.

"Why did you send Hank away?" she asked the woman in the mirror. "It's not like there's any chance of falling in love with the man, is there?"

So I panicked! she answered herself.

"What's to panic about? After all, Sally, you've got five years of heavy insulation wrapped around your heart."

I was afraid it wasn't enough.

"It's enough. Besides, if you catch yourself getting in too deep, you can always back off."

But he thinks I'm batty.

"Wrong again. He's onto your Mad Sally charade, girl. Did it ever occur to you that this is your chance to get out a bit in the world?"

But I like Hank. He deserves more than I can give him.

"You're exaggerating your worth, Sally. Hank doesn't want anything more than a temporary interlude."

This is Mad Sally you're talking to. I'd advise you to keep that in mind.

She shrugged. "Okay. So he wants a *hot* temporary interlude. What's the crime in that?"

The crime is that your experience with sex is definitely on the tepid side. Admit it, girl. You're not up to Hank's speed.

She stuck out her tongue at her reflection and turned her back on the mirror before she could decide who had won the argument. Heading down the narrow hall toward the kitchen, she wondered if perhaps her habit of talking to herself was evolving into something that should concern her.

She grinned in the darkness. "Mad Sally would never be concerned about developing a loose screw," she said aloud. "But I'd bet a psychiatrist would have a field day!"

She gave thanks that she wasn't a psychiatrist,

and flicked on the kitchen lights. It was jelly time on Blossom Lane.

Hank tried for the third time since arriving home from work to read the article about the previous night's city council meeting. It was hard going, but he was determined. The arguments about rezoning on the town's east side were important, if not exactly riveting. He owned a couple of rental properties in that area, though, so it wasn't as if this were merely an academic exercise.

If Sally Michaels would just get out of his head, he'd have a better shot at paying attention.

It had been three days since he'd tasted the sweet delights of her mouth. Three days since he'd touched skin so soft, he'd thought he was dreaming.

Three days since she'd kissed him with a passion that had hurled him into a state of arousal so fantastically exciting, he'd almost stopped breathing from the strength of it.

He crushed the newspaper between his hands. It was no use. Staring blankly at the book-lined wall of his study, he admitted that he'd been bewitched from the moment he'd first seen her. It was the only explanation that made sense.

He wanted to be her friend, as Mort Campbell was her friend. He wanted to dry her tears and make her laugh, as she had that first afternoon in her kitchen when she'd teased them about bat wings and gizzards. He wanted to know what she was hiding from that made Mad Sally an essential part of her life.

He wanted her to know she wasn't alone.

As long as he was daydreaming, Hank took his wants one step further. He wanted to share intimacies with her—*make love with her*—until the burning arousal that dragged him awake night after night was sated.

Unfortunately, it was what Sally wanted that

counted. *She* didn't want anything to do with anybody.

Back to square one. Hank shook out the wrinkled newspaper and forced himself to look at it. Time, he thought, was all he needed. In time, he'd be able to think of Sally without feeling he was missing out on an incredibly rare chance at—

"Hey, Dad! Got a minute?" Willie's face appeared over the top of Hank's newspaper, the shiner he'd got in yesterday's preseason football scrimmage developing nicely.

Hank dropped the paper on his lap and embraced the welcome distraction in a bear hug. "I see your eye is appropriately colorful," he said after Willie threw himself into an easy chair. "Does it hurt?"

"Naw," the boy drawled, then added with obvious pride, "Coach said it was the biggest black eye he'd seen since last season when Sammy Lakes smashed into that cheerleader in a practice game and she popped him."

"She didn't think it was an accident?" Hank asked, remembering his own youth, when cheerleaders had been almost as interesting as the game.

Willie shook his head. "Can't imagine why either. It's not like Sammy *wanted* to run the ball out of bounds. That fullback was going to smash him real good if he didn't."

Hank kept his own counsel on that one. At sixteen, Sammy Lakes might conceivably have had more on his mind than football. Willie, on the other hand, wasn't quite old enough to conceptualize that little fact of life.

Give him another year or two, Hank thought wryly. By then these conversations between father and son would not only be interesting but tricky as well!

"Some of the guys were talking about Mad Sally today," Willie said.

Hank's head snapped up. "What about her?"

Willie sighed. "It was really screwy. They said she

was wandering around the neighborhood right there where Blossom Lane heads out to her place."

"When?"

"Last night. I guess she scared some kids, dressed up like she was and all."

"Like what?"

His son looked at him as though he didn't like spreading tales. "In that robe thing she wears. With the hood on it that makes her look like a witch. Anyway, I guess Ernie's little sister took one look at her and screamed all the way home."

"That was it?" Hank demanded. "She was just walking around in her cloak?"

Willie shook his head. "One of the guys got close enough to hear her talking. She kept saying 'raspberry' over and over."

"Raspberry." What the hell was she up to now? Hank wondered as frustration washed over him in bludgeoning waves. Damn that woman! Didn't she realize how hard it was going to be to convince everyone she was not crazy?

His throat went dry as he realized what he'd just thought. He must be as mad as Sally even to imagine she'd want to do such a thing as plead her sanity.

"Raspberry," Willie said again. "And she kept looking under bushes." He brightened with a sudden thought. "Maybe she was hunting for raspberries?"

Hank shook his head. "Willie, whatever Sally was doing, I promise it wasn't looking for raspberries."

"How do you know that?"

"Because that answer is too easy." Throwing the unread paper onto the floor, he stood up and straightened his tie. "I'm not saying her explanation won't be logical, because it will. I'm just telling you never to expect a simple answer from her."

Willie grinned. "You're going over there to ask, aren't you?"

Hank nodded. "Among other things, Son." He thrust his arms into a cardigan sweater, then grabbed his keys and strode quickly through the house with Willie at his heels.

"Dad?"

"Hmm?"

"Are you going because she's pretty?"

Hank glanced sharply at him. He saw the wide-eyed innocence in his son's expression—and an unexpected hint of masculine understanding behind it. He'd been wrong about Sammy Lakes and the cheerleader, Hank suddenly realized. Willie had understood perfectly. He just didn't think the boy/girl thing was as important as a game.

Conversations were going to get tricky a lot faster than he'd expected. He grinned back at Willie.

"Tell your grandmother not to wait dinner."

Sally put the round loaf of sourdough bread onto the festive cake plate she'd found at the flea market the week before and stuck four tiny candles into the center. After touching a match to the wicks, she picked up the plate and tiptoed down the hall toward the living room.

The guest of honor was nibbling on the carrot appetizer she had served just moments earlier. Taking a deep breath, she breezed into the room and began to sing, "Happy Birthday to you, Happy Birthday to you, Happy Birthday, dear—"

The boom of the door gong almost made her drop the plate. The song caught in her throat as she stared at the shadowy figure on the other side of the beveled-glass door.

He'd come back!

Sally didn't even hesitate. Skipping across the room, she juggled the birthday bread with one hand and pulled open the door.

The pleasure of seeing Hank was extraordinarily intense. Her hungry gaze traveled over every inch of him, from the top of his neatly combed hair all the way down to the polished Italian loafers. She smiled at the now-familiar combination of sweater and tie—tonight's choices in shades of mauve and taupe. No one but Hank could look so elegant in what was obviously casual attire.

He looked delicious. Forgetting the quickly burning candles, she stared a while longer.

Hank saw the undisguised pleasure in her eyes and wished he could have predicted it. He would have come back sooner. Much sooner. The other night—when they'd kissed, even before that—he'd known she was attracted to him. He just hadn't believed she would ever admit it, as she was doing now with that sexy smile on her lips and a definite welcome in her gaze. He wondered how long he would have to wait for the words, but then he realized it didn't matter. As long as *he* knew, he could afford to give her the time she needed.

He stood very still, enjoying her scrutiny and returning it in full. She wore a rich deep blue caftan that lightly touched her small breasts and slim hips before drifting to the floor, leaving her arms and feet bare. Her hair was tamed tonight in long, soft waves that skimmed her shoulders. He remembered how good it had felt to grasp it . . . how exciting it had been to be that close to her.

It was incredibly difficult not to reach out and pull her into his arms.

A gust of wind blew out the candles on the cake. He smiled when he realized she hadn't even noticed.

"Sally?" he said. She didn't answer, and he decided she wasn't wearing her hearing aids. He sighed and tripled the decibels.

"*Sally!*" That certainly got her attention. Her pleasantly absorbed expression changed to one of alarmed confusion, and he watched in horrified silence as the bread slid off the plate and onto the floor.

"*What?*" she shrieked, her startled gaze alternating between the birthday bread on the floor and Hank.

"The candles," he shouted, pointing at the bread, which had miraculously landed top-side up. *"They went out!"* He watched in bemusement as Sally picked it up and dusted off the bottom before setting it back on the plate.

"So why are we yelling about it?" she demanded.

"I'm yelling because you can't hear me!" he said at the top of his lungs. *"What's your excuse?"*

"I'm yelling because you made me drop the bread!" She straightened the candles and checked that the words she'd painstakingly written in pink icing hadn't been disturbed. They hadn't.

"Bread? I thought it was a cake!" No wonder it hadn't fallen apart when it hit the floor.

"My rabbit doesn't like cake," she yelled, her lips curving into a smile. This was more fun than she'd had in years! But enough was enough. Her ears were beginning to ache.

"Hank?" she screamed one last time.

"What?"

"My hearing aids are in," she said softly.

"So why didn't—" he began in full bellow before realizing how stupid he must sound. He took deep, calming breaths and glared at her for at least a full minute before trying it again.

There was music playing in the background, something he hadn't paid attention to before. It explained why she was wearing her hearing aids. He felt like an idiot for not noticing earlier.

"So why didn't you tell me . . . Oh, never mind. It's not worth it." She was smiling. He'd only just noticed that too. He tried a different tack. "I didn't come over to yell at you."

"Who would have guessed?"

"I wanted to see you again." He could tell right away that he'd surprised her. A slight smile touched his lips as he gave her time to get used to the idea.

"Really?" Sally's heart thudded in her chest as she absorbed what he'd said. He had wanted to see her again. Perhaps all her wishful thinking over the past few days hadn't been a waste of time after all.

He nodded. "I wasn't going to tell you that. At least, not until I'd kissed you again."

The blunt admission stunned her, but she managed to muster a token resistance. It didn't seem right to cave in at the first suggestion of resuming where they'd left off.

"What makes you think I'm going to let you?"

"Let me what?" he asked, his voice low and seductive and very daring.

She couldn't resist. "Kiss me." Double dare. She stared up into eyes that darkened with her words, and was nearly overwhelmed with the realization that he was just restraining himself from kissing her at that very moment.

It was the most exciting thing she'd felt in years.

He nodded with cool confidence. "Nothing's impossible." He took the step that brought him inside. "Actually, now that I think about it, I probably *was* going to yell at you."

"Why should you come all this way just to exercise your lungs?" she asked, backing up as he took another step toward her so he could swing the door shut behind him.

"Yell is probably a misleading term," he said, tracking her step for step as she retreated farther into the room. "After Willie told me what you'd been up to last night, I decided you needed a firm reprimand."

Sally was puzzled and didn't even attempt to do more than stay out of arm's reach.

"Your excursion into the streets of Oakville," he reminded her. "Besides scaring Ernie's sister half to death—"

"I wasn't trying to scare anyone," she insisted.

"Apparently, your cloak does the job for you," he said dryly. "Must have something to do with a reputation you seem to have earned."

She grinned. "Props are everything in this business."

He scowled at her unrepentant expression. "You still haven't told me what you were doing. Willie came home with some wild story that you were peeking under bushes and chanting 'raspberry' every few feet." He brought himself to within several inches of where she'd halted her retreat. His scowl deepened. "One might almost think you'd gone out of your way to make certain there wasn't a single person in this town who doubted your reputation."

Sally looked down at the birthday bread in her hands and started to laugh. Hank was never going to live this one down, not if she could help it. Shoulders shaking, she turned the plate in her hands until he could see the words she'd written atop the bread.

"Happy Birthday, Raspberry." Hank read the words aloud before returning his puzzled stare to her face. Then he followed her gaze over her shoulder to a nearby throw rug, where an enormous white rabbit was munching on a handful of baby carrots.

"Hank," Sally said, a wicked twinkle in her eye, "say hello to Raspberry."

Five

Hank stared at the rabbit for a long moment before lifting his gaze to catch the smirk on Sally's lips. "You were chasing after a runaway rabbit," he said. It wasn't a question.

"You're pretty quick for an attorney," she said, her eyes dancing in feigned surprise. "Most people would have thought I was hunting raspberries out of season."

"That was Willie's guess," he said, grinning wryly.

She giggled. He lifted a reproving eyebrow. "You couldn't have left that damned cloak at home?" he asked.

"No."

"Because you felt compelled to bolster your reputation?"

"Because it had been raining before I went out. I didn't want to get wet." Her smile was gently admonishing. "Not everything I do is for effect."

His snort told her how much he believed her. Sally decided to pretend she hadn't heard.

"I was just going to give Raspberry his birthday bread when you arrived. Would you like to stay for the party?" She tried to sound offhand and nonchalant about the invitation so that he wouldn't realize how very much she wanted him to stay. She wasn't used to asking anything of anyone, and the threat of rejection was almost worse than the asking. Deftly avoiding his gaze, she dug her toes into the shell-pink carpet and held her breath.

The hand that captured her chin and brought her gaze in line with his put an end to her evasions. She stared up into his dark emerald eyes, and to her surprise discovered questions, not answers.

"Silent signals are sometimes louder than words," he said, his thumb caressing the line of her jaw. "What are you so afraid of that you can't look at me when you ask such a simple thing like that I stay for a party?"

"I'm not afraid," she said quickly. He didn't look as if he believed her, and she was surprised when he didn't pursue it.

"Do you really want me to stay?"

She nodded. His knuckles grazed the tender skin beneath her chin, and she almost groaned her pleasure.

"Then I will." He dropped a light kiss on her forehead before releasing his hold on her chin. "Never be afraid to be honest with me, Sally. It's much easier on the nerves if you say what you mean right at the beginning."

She stared up at him, tongue-tied and feeling completely out of her depth. There was something in what he said, though, because it gave her a degree of confidence to know he had wanted to see her again.

However, it certainly didn't prepare her for what he said next.

"I want you, Sally. But I think you've already figured that out."

Her eyes widened, then slammed shut—but not before she'd seen the honesty of his words borne out by the heated desire in his gaze. She gave a small moan and wished he wouldn't be quite so direct, at least not until she had more practice.

"Do you have more candles for the, er, bread?" he asked curiously.

"Candles?" She looked down at the four blue stubs on the bread. "Oh, yeah. Candles." She turned to go back to the kitchen, but before she'd taken two steps, his voice stopped her.

"Thank you for asking me to stay," he said. "And, Sally?"

"What?" She glanced back so that she could see his face in the fading evening light.

"Think about what I said before."

"You've said a lot of things, Hank." But she *knew* what he was referring to. He didn't say another word as she fled down the hall toward the kitchen.

How could he be so damned controlled about all this? she wondered, fuming as she emptied the box of candles onto the table. He said he wanted her in one breath, then asked about candles in the next. How was she supposed to keep up?

"It's not just that you're out of practice," she muttered under her breath. Her fingers shook as she substituted the candles and lighted the match. "Hank is playing a game you've never learned."

The truth of that stopped her in her tracks. Her relationship with her husband had never been so boldly sensual. Sex with John had been a combination of duty and an undemanding sort of need that had made their more intimate relations a comfortable interlude, if not necessarily an exciting one.

John. She wasn't supposed to think about him. He was dead, and there was nothing that could wipe away those last horrific moments together—a second in time when their complacent lives had exploded into tragedy.

Taking a deep breath, she picked up the plate and walked back down the hall to Hank.

He was waiting for her, watching as she crossed the room. She didn't meet his gaze, but Hank knew better than to expect her to. He didn't mind that she was shy of him. In fact, it was rather appealing. It made him feel as if he were the first man in her life.

There had been someone before him. How he knew that was a point for curiosity. Sally's background was a total blank to him, though he intended to remedy that. Eventually. He wasn't in a hurry. There would be time for everything.

Her tentative smile left him totally unprepared for what happened next. She took a deep breath, opened her mouth, and belted out "Happy Birthday." Much to his dismay, she warbled and wobbled through the verse without achieving a single note that wasn't flat or otherwise distorted. Even the guest of honor stopped eating his carrots and twitched his whiskers as he stared unblinkingly at Sally. When it was over—which wasn't a moment too soon as far as Hank was concerned—Sally knelt down in front of Raspberry and helped the rabbit blow out the candles.

Hank eased down onto the floor beside her and waited patiently as she tore bits of bread from the loaf and put them onto the rabbit's plate. Then he watched as Sally opened a brightly wrapped package and showed the contents to the rabbit. It was a bag of pistachio nuts, and no sooner had she untied the ribbon than Raspberry scarfed down two in very short order.

"That's enough for now," she advised, setting the bag on a nearby table. "You can have more after you finish your veggies." She scratched the rabbit between his ears and said, "You're welcome."

Hank decided that talking to animals was a step up from talking to rocks. "Does Raspberry appreciate all this fuss?" he asked.

She laughed. "This isn't fuss. This is tradition, although I'm beginning to wonder if Raspberry is less tone-deaf than I'd thought. I swear he looked like he wanted to put his paws over his ears."

He wasn't the only one, Hank thought. He glanced

up and was startled to find Sally staring at him with a decidedly reproving expression.

"I can read minds," she said threateningly, "and if you want to stay for dinner, you'll have to refrain from insulting the cook."

He grinned. "You only know what I'm thinking because it's true. And I didn't realize I was invited for dinner too."

Leaving the plate on the floor, Sally scooted away from the feasting rabbit and got to her feet. He had a point. She hadn't invited him to dinner.

But she wasn't ready to let him leave. Not yet.

She'd spent the last three days hoping against hope that he would come back. Now that he had, she wasn't about to let him leave without showing him she could be quite normal when she put her mind to it.

I want you, Sally. His words danced in her head until she was almost dizzy with excitement.

He rose to his feet with easy, unhurried movements. Tall and coordinated, she mused, and wondered why his son had fallen out of her tree. Perhaps he just hadn't inherited his father's natural grace. When Hank was standing beside her again, she repeated her invitation.

"I'd like it very much if you could stay for dinner." Then she remembered he didn't live alone and sighed. "I'm sorry, Hank. I forgot all about Willie. He must be expecting you home."

"I told Willie and Catherine not to wait dinner for me," he said, correctly interpreting her disappointment and feeling enormously pleased by it.

"Catherine?" An enormous, dark cloud appeared over Sally's horizon.

"My mother."

She cheered up considerably. "Your mother lives with you?"

He nodded but didn't elaborate. "What's on the menu?"

He was staying. She was ecstatic. "Birthday tradition requires that Raspberry get his favorite food—sourdough bread—and I get mine. You can share either."

Hank distinctly recalled that the bread had already made close acquaintance with the floor. He replied appropriately. "I'm sure whatever you're having will be fine," he said solemnly. He moved so that he was within easy touching distance of her, and was pleasantly surprised when she didn't back away.

"Are you sure you want me to stay?" he asked softly.

She didn't hesitate. "Yes. I'm sure." She lifted her gaze to his and inhaled sharply at the sensually intent expression in his eyes. "It's time."

He remained quiet, his silence prodding her to say something more. She paused for a long moment, and he realized she was deciding how much or how little to tell him. He let her get away with it, for now. He watched as her gaze wavered and then held fast to his.

"I came to Oakville five years ago," she said, "because I didn't know anybody and didn't *want* to know anybody. I have worked very hard to make sure everyone understands that."

He regarded her solemnly. "That's why I want you to be sure. It's why I've tried to stay away."

"I'm glad you came back," she said simply, then swallowed over a lump in her throat that wouldn't go away. "It's time to bend the rules a bit. I've thought about little else since the day you broke into my kitchen."

"I didn't break into your kitchen. The door was open."

"Unlocked."

"Moot point," he muttered. He didn't want to argue. He wanted to wrap his arms around her and bring her close so that she could feel what she was doing to him without even trying.

She knew he wanted her. It was time to remind her, though. He didn't want her to forget, not even for a second.

"We are going to be good together, honey," he said, gently wrapping his hands around her arms just in case she had the inclination to turn away. He wanted to watch her face. "Very good, I think."

"You're going too fast—"

"I'm being honest. Now admit that you want me too."

She nodded. She couldn't help it. It was hard not to do what he asked when he was looking at her as though she were two seconds away from getting kissed. She so very much wanted to feel his lips on hers again.

He didn't take her up on her silent offer, but went on talking in a husky voice that sent arrows of heat racing through her blood. "We can take this as fast or as slow as you want. It doesn't matter." He knew he was lying, but what the hell. He'd take it at her pace if it killed him.

"Okay." What could it possibly hurt to give in to the arousal he provoked with just a look, a touch? Would giving in to her physical desires cut her heart into ribbons?

Not as long as she didn't let it happen. She could keep her heart safe, she assured herself. For that matter, she could keep her heart out of things altogether. Somehow, by acknowledging that control, she felt capable of doing almost anything.

She held her breath and tilted her face to his. Was he finished talking yet?

Apparently not.

"Have there been any men in your life since you moved to Colorado?" he asked with quiet intensity.

"No," she said, shaking her head in confusion. "You know I don't know anyone in Oakville."

"But there's Fairview. And New York, according to Mort."

"Mort Campbell has a big mouth," she said with wry acceptance. "And the answer is still no. You're the first man I've . . . kissed . . . in five years."

Hank was curious about the years before that, but he put his questions on hold. His suspicions had been confirmed. Sally had been alone, without a man, for five years.

He'd have to be exceptionally gentle with her.

"Why now, Sally?" he asked, his mouth just inches from her ear. "Why are you changing the rules after so long?"

Her first impulse was to tell him he was asking the impossible, but she couldn't. He needed to know so that he wouldn't expect too much from her.

"Can I answer that another time?" she asked with an annoying hint of panic in her voice. Steady on, Sally, she chastised herself. There's nothing to be afraid of as long as you keep your wits about you.

"It's all right, honey," he said softly. "You can do anything you want." Lifting a hand, he fingered a soft curl that lay across her shoulder before gliding his palm up and down her bare arm.

"Anything?" The whispered word barely made it past her lips. She stood paralyzed under his light caress as her mind exploded with the implications.

"Anything." The touch of his mouth on hers was warm and firm and fleeting. But her eyes had no sooner drifted closed than it was over.

Sally was definitely miffed.

"You mentioned something about food?" he asked, and laughed when she scowled up at him.

"Now?"

"Now." Laughing again as a deep blush colored her cheeks, he turned her in the direction of the kitchen and shoved lightly between her shoulder blades. "Raspberry is going to be all done before we even get started."

Sally complied only because she had no choice.

"How hungry are you?" she asked over her shoulder as she led the way down the hall.

Hank thought about the variety of hungers assailing him as he watched the caftan shifting across her hips. He could go entirely without food, but his appetite for Sally was something he couldn't even begin to measure. Thinking that perhaps he'd made a mistake just moments ago, he gave due consideration to pulling her back into his arms.

"Hank?"

"Yes?"

"I asked how hungry are you?"

He blinked and realized they were standing in the kitchen and that Sally was having to repeat herself. It worried him, these lapses in concentration he'd been experiencing of late. It didn't bode well for an attorney if he was having trouble keeping his thoughts on track. He resolved to try harder.

It was then that he noticed the hacksaw in her hand. He cleared his throat and tried to keep an open mind. "What's that for?"

"Dinner, of course," she said, shaking her head at his hesitation. "It's not like I expected company, you know. I'll have to cut off some more, if you'll only tell me how much you want."

He leveled a hard stare at her smiling face and wondered how many years it had taken her to perfect her routine. It was really quite good. "Cut off some more *what*?"

"Salmon." Her smile full of mischief, she thrust the hacksaw into his hand and pivoted to open the freezer compartment of the refrigerator, When she pulled out a long, aluminum-wrapped object, understanding dawned on him. She tossed it with a careless thunk onto the kitchen table and grabbed a heavy wooden cutting board from the counter.

"I think I'll let you do the cutting," she said. "I wore myself out doing my own."

"I'll bet you did." He approached the table and

thumped the salmon with his fingers. "This thing is frozen solid."

She nodded. "You can have two or three if you like, but no more than an inch-and-a-half thick. I'll never get it defrosted otherwise."

Not believing for a second she'd get them defrosted at all, at least not before morning, he put down the saw and unwrapped the fish. A minor thing like frozen salmon wasn't going to deter him from accepting this dinner invitation.

"Where did you finally find Raspberry?" he asked without turning from his task.

"In the maze at the side of the house," she said, her voice laden with chagrin. "If I'd looked there in the first place, I wouldn't have had to cause such a ruckus in Oakville." Sally decided in that moment that the Fates had taken a hand, because Hank had used the incident as an excuse to return.

How much longer would it have taken otherwise? she wondered. Too long, she rather thought.

"I noticed the maze the other day," he said. "Any particular reason you had to have one in your own yard?" He didn't bother to ask if, in fact, it had been Sally's project. He couldn't imagine anyone else doing something quite so . . . unique.

"Raspberry needs exercise, but outside of an occasional hop through the neighborhood, he doesn't much care for it. He'd rather loaf around and eat." Sally poured hot water into the powder that would eventually resemble melted butter without the calories and cholesterol. Taste was purely an individual call, but she was only using it to baste the salmon, so she didn't worry.

Stirring the mixture, she continued, "When I realized he'd do just about anything for food, I thought a maze would do the trick—confuse him into running in circles as he was trying to get to the center."

"Does it work?"

"Nope. It took two years for the little branches to

grow close enough together so that he couldn't take shortcuts. By that time he'd figured out the shortest route from beginning to end. He can do it in thirty seconds flat." She sighed theatrically. "Now I'm the one getting all the exercise keeping the silly thing trimmed. I swear that rabbit laughs at me behind my back, but I haven't caught him yet."

Smiling, she grabbed a plate from the cupboard and carried it over to the table.

Hank sensed her presence just in time. He steadied his grip on the saw just as she brushed his arm slipping the plate beside the cutting board. Good thing he'd anticipated that one, he thought. Sawing off a couple of fingers would inevitably have changed the mood of the evening. The prospect was intolerable.

But it was so difficult to concentrate when she touched him.

She returned to the counter without seeming to notice his close call. "I think Raspberry was hiding because I'd slipped and mentioned giving him a bath. Anyway, when he didn't come back after his morning walk, I was afraid he'd gotten lost."

Visions of Mad Sally wandering around the neighborhood peeking under shrubs and chanting "Raspberry" drifted through his thoughts. Hank was beginning to accept that no matter what she did, everyone would continue to look to the occult or the bizarre for an explanation. How was he ever going to change that trend?

It shook him to realize that it was the second time in as many hours that he'd asked himself almost the same question. He blocked it out.

"You couldn't have worn a raincoat like normal people wear?" he asked over his shoulder, rewrapping the salmon after he'd cut off two steaks. "A yellow slicker or something ordinary?"

"Of course not," she said, laughing when he shook

his head in obvious disgust. "People expect the cloak. I couldn't disappoint them."

"I *knew* you were doing it for effect!" he exclaimed, turning to waggle the hacksaw accusingly in her direction.

"Oops." Sally grimaced at her error. Hank had certainly tripped her up on that one. Then again, maybe she'd let him do it.

It was fun teasing him about Mad Sally.

"And I suppose," he continued, "it wouldn't do to advertise that there was a beautiful brunette living at the end of Blossom Lane instead of a witch, now would it?"

"Beautiful brunette? Get your eyes checked, Hank. Willie just about fainted when he got his first look at the real me."

He turned again and stared at her until a blush colored her cheeks. "My son was terrified you were going to put a hex on him. You could have looked like Miss America and he wouldn't have noticed."

"Miss America?"

"Absolutely." He thrust the salmon back into the freezer and handed her the plate with the frozen steaks.

Sally grinned, the shoved the plate into the microwave and punched the buttons for automatic setting—Frozen Fish, Defrost. Hank was definitely good for the ego, she mused. Still, he'd never seen what she looked like upon waking.

He would, though. She couldn't lie to herself about that. The possibility of sleeping or napping with Hank brought yet another hot blush to her face, before she realized there was something else to consider here.

Hank deserved to be warned.

"When Willie fell out of the tree," she said, "I'd just gotten up from a nap." She waited until she was sure she had his attention before continuing. "I don't sleep well. I never sleep pretty. Most people in Oakville assume Mad Sally is wrinkled and ugly under that hood." She dared him to disagree. When he didn't, she went on. "For about ten minutes after I wake up, I more than fulfill their worst expectations."

"Always?"

She nodded solemnly.

He looked mildly skeptical and not at all bothered.

"Are you afraid I'll run screaming if you look less than gorgeous the morning after I make love to you?" he asked, his voice rough and husky as he pictured her mussed hair and swollen lips after a long night of his giving her pleasure.

Sally's breath caught in her throat as he crossed the three feet that separated them. She couldn't speak, especially not when he dipped his head to touch his lips to the top of her head.

"You need to get something straight, honey," he murmured. "I don't give a damn what you've suckered the people in this town into believing. It doesn't have anything to do with us."

"No?" she asked softly.

He slowly shook his head. "No. And I'm not here because I'm intrigued by Mad Sally."

She swallowed and stared into his eyes.

"I'm here because there's something about Sally Michaels that's got me twisted inside out. I intend to stick around and figure out what it is."

Sally was suddenly beset with the frightening notion that Hank was going to force a major change in her life—whether she wanted it or not.

Six

"Don't talk like that," Sally said, her voice barely a whisper. "You're scaring me."

He shook his head. "You don't scare that easy." His hands reached for hers. "You're just a little nervous because you haven't done this in a while. Trust me," he urged, his mouth a breath from hers.

His strong fingers closed over her slender ones. He stroked the soft skin between each of them before lifting her hands to his shoulders. In a seductive whisper that sensitized her lips, he suggested she find something to hang on to.

Trust me, he said. Sally couldn't think of a single reason not to. She curled her hands around his neck, discovering corded muscle that was curiously tense. If she didn't know better, she'd think he was as nervous about this as she was.

"Holding on?" he asked.

She nodded just enough so that he'd get the idea.

"Good." He teased her lips again, his mouth barely touching hers. "This is going to knock your socks off, honey."

"How do you figure that?"

He retreated an inch or so and settled a hot, sexy

stare on her face. "Remember the night in the garden when I kissed you?"

She nodded. How could he imagine she'd forget?

"It was the single most erotic moment I've ever experienced," he said, his voice a low growl that seconded his assessment. He nibbled at the corner of her mouth. "It'll be even better this time, honey. Now that we both know what we want."

She knew what she wanted, didn't she? Sally asked herself the question one final time. When the answer came back the same, she decided not to risk asking it again.

"Just one thing," she said, her breath coming fast and shallow.

"Hmm?" His lips slid across her cheek and tickled the outside of her ear.

"I'm not wearing any socks."

He chuckled and slowly lowered his head to hers.

He took possession of her mouth slowly, making certain every sensation was felt and acknowledged before going on to the next. Her lips tingled as he lightly brushed his across them. She rose onto her toes to increase the pressure, and was frustrated when he kept up the teasing caress.

He murmured something about patience and wrapped an arm around her waist so that she was crushed to his chest. Then his mouth settled firmly on hers as his hands roved the expanse of her back. She cried out as he took her bottom lip between his teeth and tugged, then moaned when his tongue laved the erotic hurt.

She slid her tongue into his mouth and stroked the raspy length of his. He became passive, and she took advantage of that to explore. She whipped her tongue across sharp, even teeth, tasted his mouth with a curiosity that was compellingly exciting. She nibbled on the tip of his tongue, then again stroked it firmly with her own.

When she sucked his tongue between her lips,

however, he took over. One hand came up to hold her head still. The other cupped her bottom and brought her hard against his heated arousal. She could feel him against her belly, and was proud and awed and thrilled by the strength of his desire. His tongue pushed inside her mouth, and retreated only to thrust into her again. She moaned and tangled her fingers in his hair.

Hard and strong, his mouth possessed hers in a vivid illustration of needs and desires that was far more intimate than the kiss they were sharing. Sally gave no thought to denying him anything he asked. She was open to his every caress, and as vulnerable to his needs as she was to her own.

Hank reluctantly lifted his mouth from hers long before he was ready. He had to; too quickly it would be too late to stop. As much as he'd been enjoying her enthusiastic response, instinct prodded him to take his time.

He wondered if she'd say anything if he got a couple of ice cubes from the freezer and shoved them down the front of his pants. She looked a bit startled when he suddenly laughed, but he didn't enlighten her. In fact, he didn't say anything at all until he was reasonably sure he had himself under control.

Staring at her face, sweetly flushed with arousal, he wanted to promise they'd be making love before the night was over. He didn't, though, because he was pretty sure that was the one thing that wasn't going to happen.

He wanted to know her better before he lost his body in hers. Taking a deep, fortifying breath, he tried to remember what had started him kissing her in the first place. Oh, yeah. Something about Mad Sally's ugly twin, as Willie would say. Hank cleared his throat and fixed a no-nonsense expression on his face.

"I don't want to hear any more nonsense about the uglies," he said sternly. "Do you understand?"

Sally nodded and sighed. Well, she thought, she'd *tried* to warn him.

The microwave binged, and she spun out of his arms. It was a relief and a letdown all at once, but she convinced herself she needed the space.

She couldn't think, much less cook, when he was holding her. And while she was pretty sure she didn't want to think, cooking was another matter. She was hungry. Pulling out the thawed salmon steaks, she transferred them to the range grill and tossed on a third from the refrigerator.

"These steaks won't be terrific," she warned, "but a quick defrost is better than soiled sourdough."

"Don't think I don't appreciate that," he said solemnly. He pulled out a chair from the kitchen table and straddled it. Watching her move around the kitchen, he wondered if she cooked for herself every night . . . or if tonight was a special occasion.

It was special for him.

"Why is a pure white rabbit called Raspberry?" he asked after she'd cleaned the asparagus, turned the steaks, fixed the salad, and attended to all the other dinner chores without once looking his way.

"Excuse me?"

"The name. There's got to be a story there." Knowing Sally, she'd make up one if he gave her half a chance. He didn't care.

Sally was fascinating no matter what she did or said.

She checked the stove one more time, then leaned against the counter and actually looked at him. He took a sip of the wine she'd poured him during his salmon-cutting task and rested his chin on the back of the chair. He was ready to be entertained.

He wasn't disappointed.

"Indian legend has it that when a baby is born, the mother goes out of the tepee and names the child after the first thing she sees."

Hank couldn't have moved if he'd wanted. He was

having too much fun watching Sally invent her story. At least, he *thought* it was a fabrication. She had a certain look about her that made him imagine she was putting him on. That was okay. Watching her was all he wanted to do, regardless of the excuse.

"There was an Indian boy," she went on, "who asked his mother why his sister was called Running Brook." Sally kept her voice low and melodic, because she knew proper storytelling demanded proper atmosphere.

"'Because I went out of the tepee and saw a beautiful running brook,' said his mother."

"'And what about Soaring Eagle?' the young boy asked."

"'I walked outside the morning after your brother was born and lifted my face into the warm heat of the sun and saw an eagle swoop and soar down from a mountain peak far away,' she explained, a smile in her eyes at the memory of that beautiful moment.

"The young Indian boy was silent for the longest time. Finally, his mother asked, 'Does that answer your question, Frog with a Wart?'"

Laughter burst from Hank, but he didn't take his gaze off Sally. He was enjoying her own radiant expression too much to look away. He watched as she tended the steaks on the grill, and was still chuckling when she put place mats, napkins, and flatware on the table.

"And Raspberry is named after . . . ?"

"A particularly good batch of raspberry jelly I'd put up the morning I brought him home," she said, serving dinner onto the plates she'd taken from the cupboard.

"It's a good thing you weren't making crab-apple jelly that day," he said, pulling out a chair and holding it for her. He managed to stifle his disappointment when she slipped into the seat without touching him even once.

She grinned and picked up her fork. "If I'd adhered

strictly to legend, Raspberry would be named 'Parking Meter,' and your son's story would have been substantially more interesting."

Hank laughed, but Sally didn't. She was too busy paying attention to little details that hadn't registered before, things like how his eyes lightened when he was enjoying himself. She noted the laugh lines at the corners of those eyes and knew for a fact that he hadn't got them by squinting. Hank Alton was a man who liked to smile.

Under the bright kitchen lights they ate slowly and talked without any sense of urgency. There was so much to say, to learn. But it was apparent from the beginning that neither wanted to rush.

It shouldn't have felt so comfortable, Sally mused, having Hank sit across the table from her. But it did. He was a man about whom she knew so little . . . a man who had kissed her and promised so much more.

Her senses vibrated in anticipation of what was to come.

She thought she might have been at least a tiny bit bewitched by the emerald gaze that never seemed to stray far from her face. And she couldn't help her smile as she closed her mouth over her fork. Hank would have been amused to discover she considered him capable of witchcraft.

They exhausted the subjects of Raspberry, Willie's black eye, and Sally's penchant for small, fast cars. She teased him about the macho four-wheeler he drove, and he demanded to know how she got around Colorado in winter when the drifts were six feet deep.

"I'm terrific at putting on chains," she boasted. "And besides, little cars are hot stuff on snow-packed roads. The only problem was getting out of the garage, but now that I've got a snowblower, I've got four wheels that love the white stuff."

She left out the part about having to negotiate the private access road—a quarter-mile long and not on the county's list for maintenance. She also didn't tell him about the four-wheel-drive pickup she kept for the really bad days. Mere details, she told herself. He couldn't possibly be interested in everything.

Hank strained to keep from asking what the *hell* she was doing in snow country without proper transportation. The only thing that kept him in check was knowing that, in a few weeks, he'd have the edge to make changes.

Sally wasn't going to drive that hot little car anywhere once the snow began to fly. He'd make sure of it.

Oblivious to his train of thought, Sally pushed her plate aside and picked up her wine. "Have you always practiced law in Oakville?"

He shook his head. "Until about two years ago I worked in Denver. Then I decided to get us out of the city, so I opened up my own office. I retained my partnership standing in the Denver firm, though, so most of my cases still originate from there."

"That must make for a tiring commute," she said. Denver was almost an hour's drive from Oakville—more in winter, when the roads were snow-packed and treacherous.

He shrugged. "I don't go up unless I'm due in court or need to see people. And I've got a clerk in Denver who sends me pretty much what I need, so I can do most of the work here."

"And when you have to be gone, your mother runs things," she said, a prick of envy catching her by surprise. She ignored it.

"Catherine runs things whether I'm here or not," he said. A smile lighted up his eyes. "From the moment I convinced her to come to Oakville with us, she's been in charge."

"Why do you call her by her first name?" It was the second time that night he'd done it. Sally thought it was a bit odd, but then, she'd lost her parents when she was a child. What did she know about family life?

"It was something I did to make her crazy when I was growing up. By the time I got over the rebellious-teenager phase, she'd gotten used to it." He shrugged matter-of-factly. "It stuck."

"And Willie calls her . . . ?"

"Mom." He understood her puzzled glance. "Catherine is really the only mother he's ever known." Hank hesitated, then decided to tell her the rest of the story. She'd have to know about Sandra sooner or later. "Willie's mother deserted him right after he was born. Our marriage was defunct two months after the ceremony. She went off to Nevada and got a quickie divorce. I was thrilled to pay for it. The only time I saw her after that was when she dropped by to hand over my son."

"She didn't want him?"

"No."

Sally was stunned by the brutality of that act of desertion. How could a mother abandon her own child?

A child. Years ago, she had longed for a baby. But those dreams had died with her husband. She hadn't thought about it since.

"Let's not talk about Sandra anymore," said Hank, pushing his plate aside. "My life with her was over a long time ago. The only good thing that came from that marriage is Willie."

Sally had no doubt that he meant every word of it. Relegating Willie's mother to past history, she went back to asking about his job.

They drank a little more wine, and he told her about a few of the cases he was working on. She fixed coffee, and they sipped it slowly as she listened to Hank's sometimes funny, sometimes heartbreaking stories of past cases.

He even told her about the ones he'd lost. She listened with rapt attention, interrupting with so many questions that Hank finally said he'd had enough. She hadn't, but she gave in gracefully and cleared the table. When he tried to help her with the dishes, she scolded and pushed him back to his chair. He was a guest, she reminded him. Her first in years. She wanted to do things right.

Then she said he could do them the next time. By himself.

Eventually, they drifted out to the living room, where Raspberry had fallen asleep in front of his plate. Hank settled into a comfortably padded chair while Sally snuggled into a corner of the sofa, her bare toes hidden beneath the caftan. He watched her carefully without staring. He didn't want her to feel as if he were peering into her soul—even though he was trying to do precisely that.

It was dark out when he casually asked her about her own work, darker yet when the conversation turned to the homeless shelter in Denver.

He was intrigued by her job, and could tell that she was happy doing it. As a consulting editor for a major book publisher, she worked out of her home, traveling to the New York office when necessary. She worked with real authors and real books, ushering their manuscripts through various stages of preparation. She was intricately involved with the process right up to the moment when thousands or tens of thousands or—when they got really lucky—hundreds of thousands of copies rolled off the presses. Some books were battles, and others were nothing but joy from beginning to end.

Hank got the impression the challenges were as much fun as the shoo-ins.

He was surprised that she found any time at all for the soup kitchen. She laughed and told him that wasn't work at all. The time she spent there tapped entirely different talents.

"Mostly, I just help in the food line," she said, leaning forward to set her coffee on the low table that separated them. "And dishes. I'm great at scouring industrial-sized pots."

"And you spend hours making jelly," he reminded her.

"That too. I have to admit that by the time that tree is finished dropping fruit for the year, I'm a bit sick of the whole thing."

He watched as she stretched her clasped hands high over her head and yawned. Satisfaction eased through him. He'd deliberately kept her talking, filling in conversational lulls so that she wouldn't have time to worry about what to say . . . or when he was going to take her into his arms again. It had paid off. Sally had truly relaxed after a while, gradually opening up under his delicate questioning. To avoid jostling her receptive mood, he'd side-stepped anything and everything to do with Mad Sally. That could come later, when she trusted him enough to offer it without asking.

All in all, Sally had revealed more than she realized—much more than she'd intended, he was convinced. But then, she hadn't had a chance against the skills he'd perfected over years of court-room engagements.

He wanted to learn everything there was to know about her. What he'd learned in the last few hours not only served to whet his appetite for more, it confirmed what he'd suspected all along. He wasn't just attracted to Sally. Something much deeper than simple lust made him crazy with the need to see her again.

He wanted to make her a part of his life. He needed to be a part of hers.

He wanted her for his wife.

For a man who had never considered marrying again, Hank was oddly comforted rather than shocked by the notion of spending the rest of his life with a woman he'd only just met. Once he'd had a few moments to think about it, he felt totally exhilarated.

He was also very determined to make the idea a reality.

He smiled and put his empty coffee cup down beside hers. "I've never had a woman fall asleep on me before," he said wryly, then stood up and did a little stretching himself. "At least, not *before* I made love to her."

He stopped stretching and looked at her closely. "I can't wait to see what you do after I make love to you, Sally. Will you stretch and yawn like you're doing now? Or will you just snuggle against me and go to sleep in my arms?" He cocked his head and appeared to consider the options. After a long moment during which she just stared at him with eyes wide open in stunned disbelief, he shook his head and smiled. "I guess I'll just have to wait and see."

Sally was suddenly more awake than she'd been in her entire life. And she was just a little nervous. A *lot* nervous, she amended. How could she have relaxed to the point where she'd almost forgotten what he wanted from her?

"Sally?"

Her face flamed, but she met his heated gaze without flinching. "It's late, honey. And I've got a full day in court tomorrow."

Why was that the last thing she'd expected him to say? She stared at him without comprehending.

"I'm trying a case here in Oakville," he went on. "I want to run over my notes before morning." He smiled and held out his hand. "Walk me to the door?"

"But—"

"But what, Sally?" he asked gently, walking around the coffee table to pull her to her feet. "Don't you think it's time I left?"

"Of course it is," she snapped, avoiding his hand and slipping around the other side of the table. Dammit, she thought. She wished he'd quit saying things that made her heart practically jump out of her chest! Swearing under her breath, she almost tripped over Raspberry, who was lying passed out in her path, stepping on his plate instead.

It didn't stop her from beating Hank to the door.

"Why do I get the impression you're just a touch vexed with me?" he asked, curling his fingers around hers to prevent her from opening the door. With his other hand he tugged at her shoulder until she was backed against his arm. "Was it because I mentioned making love to you?"

"You're doing it again!" she wailed. "Can't you get it through your head that I'm not used to men who talk like that?"

He smiled tolerantly. "You're not used to men at all, from what you've told me." His hand stroked the line of her shoulder, drifting upward to catch her chin in his fingers. "And I wouldn't talk like that if I didn't think you liked it."

She moaned against his lips, which were teasing the corners of her mouth, and tried to catch them with her own. His laughter was soft, his breath a hot invitation she was fast becoming addicted to.

"Do you like it, Sally?" he asked, his mouth evading hers as he tracked a wet path across her cheek. "Doesn't it excite you to know I want you so badly that I can't stop myself from talking about it?"

"Well . . . um . . . I think—" She swallowed and tried to concentrate. "I just think you shouldn't—"

"Don't lie to me, Sally." His mouth covered hers just moments before his tongue prodded her lips into parting beneath his. He explored her mouth for a moment before adding, "Remember what I said about being honest. Just because we're talking about something as intimate as making love doesn't mean we can't say what we're thinking."

"It'll take me a while to get . . . used . . . to it," she whispered, trembling as his hand grazed the side of her breast. It was a touch so fleeting, she wouldn't have believed it was on purpose if she hadn't seen the arousal that flared for a moment in his eyes.

"Then come out with me tomorrow, and I'll try to behave."

"Come out?" she asked. He nodded, then his mouth moved gently on hers, leading her into a kiss that soon had her clinging to him. After what seemed like an eternity, he raised his head, and she was forced to meet his gaze.

"Please come out to dinner with me," he said softly. "I want to be with you again."

She took a deep breath and agreed, wondering if he could possibly realize what an enormous step she was taking. "I think I'd like to do that very much," she said solemnly.

He grinned and nodded as though he already knew that, but kissed her again before she could call him on it. When he finally said good night and left, she decided he deserved a little arrogance.

His kisses were awesome.

Seven

"Hank, I'd like to make love. Now, before we have dinner," she said firmly. "Do you mind?"

Sally pulled the bottle of white wine out of the freezer and popped it into the refrigerator.

"No, that isn't quite right," she said, shaking her head in frustration as she slammed the door. Multiple layers of grape-colored chiffon swirled around her knees as she walked across the floor to the cabinet where she kept her good crystal. She pulled down two glasses and leaned back against the counter. A glass in each hand, she said it again—but just a little bit differently.

"Hank, if you don't mind, I think I'd like to make love before we go out." Her brow furrowed. No. Somehow, it was lacking something.

All her attempts had been lacking something. That was why it was seven o'clock already and she was still searching for the perfect words. Hank was due any second, and she was getting ready to panic.

He'd said he spoke honestly about making love with her because he thought it excited her. Did the reverse hold true? In the long hours of the night she'd lain awake determined to be honest and straightforward with him . . . and anything else he wanted her to be. She was perfectly aware that being with Hank was more important to her well-being than just about anything in her world.

She honestly wanted to be his lover.

Sally smiled across the room to where Raspberry was munching on a snack of lettuce and raw radishes. Being with Hank was akin to throwing caution to the wind, she realized, but even better.

She didn't have to be cautious about entering into a relationship with him, because he wanted the same thing out of it as she did. He'd been open about desiring her, completely up-front with his intentions. Once she had got over the initial shock, she'd realized their goals were uniquely matched.

It put a whole new perspective on things, she mused. Neither of them was interested in pursuing matters of the heart. Considering Hank's forthright manner, he would have said something if he expected more than simple physical intimacy. In that context Sally was content with her analysis of the situation. They could spend time together without worrying about mating rituals. Such rites could ultimately destroy otherwise perfectly good relationships by binding together two people who had no more interest in each other than the most basic of all urges.

She and Hank would mate, but not for life. This thing between them was a passing attraction. That was why she could allow it to happen.

For the moment, though, Sally was honestly convinced that she'd rather eat bat wings than sit through a long dinner with Hank without first becoming his lover.

Perhaps she should use force. She cleared her throat and imagined the scene. Hank would ring the bell. She would open the door, grab hold of his necktie, and—

The door gong interrupted her strategy. "Rats," she growled, and fled down the hall on high, strappy sandals.

This was it. *Think, Sally!* But it was too late. She was at the door and still hadn't made up her mind, when she noticed there were two bodies, not one, on the other side. There were also two wineglasses in her hands. The asymmetry of the moment didn't appeal to her at all.

For the first time all day Sally quit worrying about how she'd phrase her proposition to Hank. She wondered instead what on earth he was doing on her doorstep with another woman. Her first date in Oakville, she mused, and he brought a spare partner. Not a good start. She carefully put the glasses down on the table next to the door and wiped her hands on her skirt.

She opened the door.

Hank's gaze swept from the top of her sleeveless dress, past the belted waist, down to her feet, and back to her face. He did it a second time without uttering a word. Sally felt her nerves tingle under the sensual approval in his stare and gave serious consideration to a turn of phrase she'd thrown out at two o'clock. She could just picture it. *Hank, won't you come in and take your clothes off so we can get this out of the way? May I help you with your tie?*

Pangs of jealousy spurred the impulse to blurt out the provocative words. Sally did *not* enjoy seeing another woman with Hank.

Restraint narrowly governed the situation. Nevertheless, Sally kept her mouth shut—just in case the words slipped past her better judgment. The three adults stared at each other until the only one with any obvious training in etiquette took charge.

"Good evening, Ms. Michaels," the other woman said. "I'm Catherine Alton, Hank's mother."

It wasn't until that moment that Sally realized the woman standing before her was clearly several years older than Hank. She carried it well, Sally thought, with her auburn hair free of gray and her face relatively bereft of the signs of age. They were there, though, if you looked hard—a few shallow lines leading outward from her eyes, the barest suggestion of similar lines across her forehead.

Sally decided she didn't want to look very hard. She said "Hello," smiling with relief as she congratulated herself on a narrow escape. It would have been humiliating to blurt out the provocative invitation with Hank's mother in the audience.

Catherine Alton glanced despairingly at her son and said, "I'm sorry if he seems to have forgotten his manners, but you know how it is with children these days. In one ear and out the other. I swear I taught him the word 'hello' long before he was out of short pants."

Sally giggled and took the hand Mrs. Alton offered. Then she led the older woman into the house without a second glance at the man on the front stoop. "You don't have to apologize for him," Sally said with teasing aplomb. "It's a pleasant change from having him yell at me."

"You yell at her?" Catherine turned to her son, eyebrows lifted in shock.

"Now and then."

Sally whirled and caught Hank in the act of scowling at Catherine. Then he bent down to plant a chaste kiss on Sally's cheek. "I wouldn't be so tongue-tied if you didn't look so incredibly . . . gorgeous," he said huskily.

She let her gaze rest on his mouth for a long moment before taking a deep breath. She wanted a real kiss.

He chuckled and murmured, "Later." Then he cleared his throat and added, "We're dropping Catherine off at the library for a meeting on our way to dinner. I didn't think you'd mind."

Why don't you give her the keys and we'll just stay here and order pizza when we get hungry . . . if we get hungry? No, Sally told herself, that wouldn't do at all. Catherine Alton might not be amused. Besides, there wasn't a pizza man in all of Oakville who would deliver to Mad Sally's lair. She'd tried it before.

"I've got a bottle of wine cooling. . . ." she began.

"I'm not going to stay," Catherine said firmly. "I wouldn't have even come to the door except that I didn't believe Hank when he told me your pet rabbit is bigger than a cocker spaniel."

"He lied," Sally said cheerfully. "Under all that fur Raspberry couldn't possibly be any bigger than a poodle."

"A large poodle," Hank said.

"Medium." Grinning, she excused herself and made a quick trip to the kitchen. As she'd expected, Raspberry hadn't moved. He wouldn't, not as long as there was still food to be had. Scooping him up with only a small grunt from the exertion, Sally carried him back down the hall.

"Oh, my." Catherine tentatively reached out a hand and patted Raspberry on the head. "He looks like quite a handful."

"Armful, actually," Sally said. "Try scratching between his ears, Mrs. Alton."

"It's Catherine, and are you sure he won't mind?"

"Mind?" Sally laughed. "Outside of eating, being scratched between his ears is his favorite thing."

Catherine did as Sally suggested and was delighted when Raspberry took an interest in her efforts. Her strokes became firmer, and she laughed when Raspberry twitched his whiskers and nuzzled her fingers. Sally held the almost purring rabbit until her arms began to tire. When she finally set him on the floor, Raspberry shuffled back toward his food bowl.

"A charming pet," Catherine said. "Does he sleep inside?"

Sally nodded. "Raspberry is house-trained. He used to sleep with me, until he got too fat to jump onto the bed."

"And now?"

"He's got a basket. It's not so much that I mind lifting him onto the bed, but he's too afraid to jump off now, and if he needs to 'go' in the middle of the night—"

"We have a dinner reservation," Hank interrupted before the conversation deteriorated any further. "What do you say we get moving?"

Sally grinned and allowed herself to be hustled out the door, grabbing her cloak on the way. She ignored Hank's grunt of disapproval.

"It's not cold enough for this," he muttered as he nevertheless settled it around her shoulders.

Sally agreed, but wisely didn't mention the security-blanket aspects of the infamous cloak. Her first night out in Oakville certainly deserved some sort of talisman, she decided.

Walking down the path between Catherine and Hank, she spotted a sleek black Jaguar sedan parked in the lane.

"Where's the truck?" she asked.

He smiled and helped Catherine into the backseat. A hand riding at the small of her back, he guided Sally around to the passenger door. "Willie thought the car was more your style than the four-by-four."

"Willie has good instincts."

"Willie gets his manners from me," Catherine said blithely. "Where are you going for dinner?"

"Le Casa di Antoine." Hank started the car and headed down Blossom Lane toward town. "It's the best restaurant in Oakville," he added, reaching across the console to snag Sally's hand. "I was lucky to get a table."

"Le Casa di Antoine? Aren't there a couple of languages mangled there?" Sally asked. Her hand felt pleasantly warm in his grasp. She very much enjoyed touching Hank, even in such an innocent way as holding hands.

She wondered if he remembered his mother was in the backseat.

Hank nodded in answer to her question. "The food is a rather creative mixture of French, Italian, and Spanish. I think you'll like it." With a slight pressure he arranged her fingers on the gearshift and curled his own around hers. When he changed gears, she sighed a gentle breath of contentment.

"You've never heard of it?" Catherine asked from the backseat.

"I don't get out much," Sally said with a straight face. The word "never" would have better described her sojourns into town. Tonight was going to be a first for Mad Sally.

It almost shocked her to realize she wasn't the least bit uneasy. Being with Hank, facing the world. Both seemed to be the most natural thing in the world.

"That's right," Catherine said, a note of speculation in her voice. "I've always wondered why you kept so much to yourself."

"It was peaceful," Sally murmured. *Was?* she repeated silently. Well, it made a certain kind of sense that she'd speak in the past tense about her life as a hermit.

It was becoming clear to her that in accepting Hank's presence in her life, she'd opened the door to a whole new series of experiences. Getting to know Oakville was just one of them.

She was looking forward to it. But how would Oakville react to Mad Sally?

"Why did you let all those rumors get started?" Catherine asked.

"The ones about the witch or the madwoman?" Sally glanced over her shoulder and shared a mischievous smile with the other woman.

"Both, I imagine," Catherine said. "From what I understand, you've never done anything to discourage either. Mad Sally is altogether a fearsome character. Why did you allow things to grow so far out of proportion?"

"Umm—"

"For that matter," Catherine continued without missing a beat, "how did you manage to keep the myth going all these years?"

"What makes you think it's all a myth?" Sally managed to insert.

"Don't be silly. Of course it's a myth," the older woman said in a no-nonsense voice. "I mean, you're a perfectly lovely young woman. Did you have to make up your face with warts and things just to scare the kids once in a while?"

Sally was wondering if she should confess in three easy sentences about how she'd stumbled upon the concept of Mad Sally, when Hank intervened.

"Leave it alone, Catherine," he said softly.

"I don't mind, Hank," Sally said quickly. It was a good thing Catherine hadn't been around when Mad Sally first emerged, she thought. Simple theatrics wouldn't have been enough to fool this woman.

Hank shot Sally a look that made her bite her tongue. "Don't you think perhaps I deserve to know the answers to those questions first?"

"Don't talk to Sally like that, Hank," Catherine said imperiously. "You'll make her nervous before you even get to that restaurant . . . and it's going to be bad enough once you do get there. Everyone is going to want to meet her, and what are you going to say when they ask where she lives?" Catherine stopped for a breath before finishing. "Truly, Hank. How are you going to explain that Sally is from Oakville without revealing she lives in the house at the end of Blossom Lane? This town is too small for you simply to introduce her as Sally Michaels and get away with it. Is that any way to spend your first date?"

Hank pulled up in front of the library without answering and helped his mother from the car. She had a ride home, she assured them, rapping on Sally's window in farewell. And she'd pick up Willie from the neighbors on her way. Hank slid back into the driver's seat and recaptured Sally's hand.

"Are you nervous about the restaurant?" he asked with sudden concern. Le Casa di Antoine was the only restaurant in Oakville, if one didn't count the handful of diners and fast-food franchises. He'd forgotten that it was sure to be filled with acquaintances and friends—*curious* acquaintances and friends.

It was a major blunder. But then, neither did he want to drive all the way to Fairview or even Denver. He wanted to spend the evening with her, and not in the front seat of a car.

He hadn't stopped to think what Sally might have preferred.

Sally swallowed back a wave of butterflies. Of course she was nervous, but not about eating in a big, noisy restaurant. She did that all the time in New York. There were other things on her mind—like was she doing the right thing? Was she mad to think she could enter into a relationship with Hank and then walk away with her heart untouched? She decided to avoid his question as well as her own.

"I like your mother," she said.

"She likes you. Are you nervous about the restaurant?" *Or was she frightened of being alone with him?* His heartbeat tripped as he considered the possibility. But the lawyer in him rejected it in the next second. Sally hadn't been frightened of him last night when they'd been truly alone.

She'd been excited, responsive . . . and as sensually eager for his kisses as he'd been for hers.

"How can you tell she likes me?" she asked quietly.

"She said she'd pick up Willie."

"How does that translate to Catherine liking me?"

"If she'd wanted, she could have figured out a way to make me do it." He turned her hand palm up and began to trace tiny circles at the center.

"This way," he went on, "we won't have to rush through . . . anything." He felt with enormous satisfaction a faintly perceptible whiplash from the tremor that surged through her. He hadn't been mistaken at all.

"Sally?"

"Hmm?"

"Tell me what you want."

Her gaze fell to his fingers as they continued to circle her open palm. It was such a simple thing, she mused. Anyone watching might have thought it an innocent caress.

She knew better. With every circuit of his fingers her breathing grew more ragged. Lightning-fast darts of arousal made direct hits where she was the most vulnerable. Her breasts began to swell. She could feel them against the silk teddy beneath her blouse, her nipples hard and peaked. Heat built at the juncture of her thighs, a slow, wet heat that she could no more control than she could take back her hand.

"Look at me, Sally," said Hank, cupping her chin when she appeared not to have heard. He waited patiently as she focused on his face. The bemusement in her eyes was an enormous reward for the simple caress.

He'd never known a woman so phenomenally responsive, he realized. He wondered if she was as sensitive everywhere, or if there were certain places that were even more susceptible to an erotic caress. Stifling a groan of anticipation, he looked forward to finding them all.

"Yes or no?" he asked. "Do you want to go to the restaurant?" He silently prayed her answer would be no. Oakville could wait until tomorrow to meet Mad Sally. Tonight, he wanted her for himself.

"You've already booked the table," she said in a small voice.

"I'll call."

"You haven't eaten."

"Neither have you," he murmured, his mouth hovering just above hers. "Tell me what you want," he commanded for the second time.

Honesty, he'd said. In all things. Sally struggled with the words that were at once shockingly blunt and excitingly provocative, until she gave up the fight and surrendered to her instincts.

"Hank, I'd like to make love. Now, before we have dinner," she said, her earlier bravado giving way to a husky plea. "Do you mind?"

Hank didn't mind at all. He kissed her once, lightly, then released her hand to shift gears. As he steered the powerful car through a U-turn and headed back toward Blossom Lane, he remembered how soft and warm she was . . . and that he could reach out and touch her if he only dared.

He didn't. He couldn't, not and drive in any sort of responsible fashion.

"Hank?"

"Hmm?"

"The first couple of times you came over, I told you to go away."

"That's true." He kept his smile to himself. He'd wondered how long it would take for her to begin to look for answers.

"I've never figured out why you kept coming back to see me."

"I know you haven't," he said, but didn't offer to tell her why. She wouldn't believe it if he told her.

"Is it because you wanted to make love with me?"

"It's not that simple."

"Then why?"

He shook his head. "You have to find your own answer to that one. And while you're trying to puzzle it out, why don't you ask yourself why you let me."

Hank took the key from her fingers and shoved it into the lock, because her hands were shaking too much to be of any help. He wasn't doing much better. But then, he'd never expected Sally to take him at his word and be so wonderfully candid about what she wanted. At least, he hadn't expected it so soon.

I'd like to make love now. . . . Do you mind? He was enchanted by her sweet appeal, aroused by the sincerity of her simple words.

He'd almost told her then that he loved her, loved her for the way she wasn't afraid to say the words she knew would please him. But that was just one of the reasons he'd fallen in love, a minor thing when compared to the way she'd stolen his heart with her smile, his soul with her laugh.

He didn't tell her that he loved her because she wouldn't have believed him. Not yet.

The key finally turned in the lock, and he pulled her behind him into the house. Tossing her cloak in the direction of the coat tree without caring whether or not it caught, he gathered her in his arms and touched her lips with his.

It had been an eternity since he'd really kissed her. He couldn't wait.

He didn't tease her with his kiss as he'd been known to do before. Sally had no sooner absorbed the slight weight of his mouth than he increased the pressure, forcing her lips to part beneath his. His tongue shot past her teeth, rasping along hers, entreating her to join in the suggestive play.

She complied with enthusiasm. Slipping her arms around his neck, she played as though this were the only game she knew. Her tongue followed his in retreat, tasting the seductive flavor of his mouth, testing his vulnerabilities. The roof of his mouth was ticklish, she discovered. She laved his lips with the tip of her tongue, then nipped and bit at his when he tried to do the same to her. There was no pain in these forays. There was only pleasure, the kind that is shared and celebrated.

Sally held nothing back and learned something

with each new kiss. Their breathing became deep and uneven, their need for air a lesser necessity than the touch of their mouths. Her chest was heaving when Hank took pity on her and slid his lips across her cheek to explore the tender skin in front of her ear.

Laughter caught in her throat because he'd finally discovered one of her ticklish spots. He paid her back in full.

"What about your hearing aids?" he asked, his voice a soft caress. "Can you keep them in for a while?"

"Why?"

"Because I want to whisper erotic things in your ear as I'm making love to you," he said, his arms loosing their granitelike clutch around her shoulders. He lifted a hand to brush the hair back from her ear, so that he could better see the tiny mechanism. "It'll make more of an impact if you can hear them."

She blushed, then did it again when he gave her a murmured sample of what he meant.

"Well?" His lips explored the soft skin behind her ear as he waited patiently for her answer, and he felt her quiver when he drew his tongue along the same path.

"They can stay in," she said, panting, her fingers digging into the rippling muscles of his shoulders. "Just don't get them wet." When he laughed, she knew he'd heard her.

"You can take them out another time," he said, being careful not to get his tongue too close to the inner curve of her ear. "We'll see if you like it better one way or the other."

Sally laughed breathlessly, and wondered why she'd never considered the amusing aspects of hearing aids.

"Does Raspberry need to take a walk or anything?" he asked, returning to nibble on her lips.

She smiled into his mouth. "He'll be fine." She ran

a hand across his shoulder to the nape of his neck, then back again. "Anything else?"

"What are the chances you'll get pregnant?" he asked, fully expecting the shock wave that rippled through her body. Her reaction didn't disappoint him, and he had to smile at the expression in her eyes. She really wasn't very good at hiding anything, especially when the subject was just a tad personal.

"Pregnant?"

He nodded. "It sometimes happens when people make love. I've brought something. I just want to know if I need to use it."

She hadn't thought about that at all! "I don't use anything," she said morosely, then did a quick calculation in her head. "But the timing is good. I must have ovulated early last week."

"You're sure?" he pressed, brushing his lips across her temple.

She thought again. "I'm sure."

"Good." He lifted her palm to his mouth and drew a circle with his tongue. He wouldn't have minded at all if she conceived this first time they made love, but that was purely selfish thinking.

He wanted the decision to be conscious, and not an accident of fate.

Most of all, though, he wanted her to know that he loved her before things were complicated by a pregnancy. Drawing her close to stand between his parted legs, he cushioned his rigid manhood against her belly and let a groan of pleasure escape his lips.

Sally thought her heart was going to stop. She could feel him hard against her, the power of his arousal luring her deeper and deeper into the sensual whirlwind he'd introduced with his kisses. His breath heated her palm, and again she felt his tongue doing totally insane things she never would have imagined could be erotic.

They were.

When he sucked her fingers into his mouth, one by

one, she nearly fell off her high heels. Only the hard pressure of his arm at her back kept her standing.

Tremors chased through her body, one on the tail of another and yet another, when he asked her to point to her room. She managed to do that, just barely. He thanked her in a voice that was sexily formal, and kissed her just once, very lightly. Then he slipped his arms beneath her shoulders and knees and lifted her across his chest. He kissed her again, a little harder this time.

She liked it when he kissed her like that and told him so.

He thanked her again, and told her to put her arms around his neck. He didn't want to drop her.

She wasn't at all worried, but she did it anyway. Being carried by Hank made her feel fragile and pampered—two things she wasn't accustomed to feeling.

He made her feel incredibly special.

He made her feel alive.

Eight

Balancing Sally high against his chest, Hank flicked on the bedroom light and took a quick survey of the room. Bed, chair, dresser, fireplace. All the basics.

His mouth touched hers in a quick caress, and he kicked the door shut. "To keep out the rabbit," he said.

"Raspberry can't jump onto the bed," she reminded him, her mouth opening on his neck just above his collar.

"I'm not in the mood to take chances. Besides, I'm not entirely convinced I'll make it that far. We might have to make do with the floor." He kissed her lips. "Or the wall. I'm not picky."

She laughed. It never occurred to her that he might be serious.

He eased his arms from beneath her knees, allowing her lower body to slide down his in slow motion. Her thighs framed his solid arousal, the thin silk of her skirt no barrier to the honesty of his body's physical response to hers. She moaned as he held her there for a moment, luxuriating in his strength, the powerful evidence of his need.

Her feet finally touched the ground, and she was suddenly conscious that the full skirt of her dress hadn't followed her downward path. It was bunched at her thighs, just above the tops of her stockings.

She tried to push it down. He captured her hand and returned it to his shoulder. "Leave it, honey," he said. "There's no place for modesty here."

"Maybe I just don't want it all wrinkled," she countered, fingering the knot of his tie and wondering abstractly if he'd take it off before he made love to her.

She'd never seen him without one, she realized. Standing on tiptoe and wrapping her fingers around his tie for balance, she nibbled on his earlobe.

Ties had their uses, she decided as her tongue speared deep into his ear. Then her teeth latched onto the lobe again, harder this time. More demanding.

He barked a short laugh and pulled the elastic waistband of her skirt over her hips, until the skirt and her slip were a puddle of color around her ankles. "If you'll let go of my ear, I'll pick those up," he said, gentlemanly instincts momentarily overcoming his preferences. He would have happily let her chew on his ear all night.

Sally decided that wrinkles weren't so important after all. Her change of mind was a direct result of the firm hand that slid across her hip and around to where her exposed thighs rubbed against the soft wool of his slacks. His fingers made a slow investigation of the bare skin above the stockings, slipping beneath the silken garters that held them in place.

A mad heat surged through her—mad because she'd never known that a sane person could be totally oblivious to any sensation or occurrence that wasn't sensual and erotic. She forgot all about the skirt and everything else as his mouth found hers in a consuming kiss, and his hands delved beneath the lace and silk that hid her feminine secrets. She clung to his shoulders, losing herself in the taste of him . . . sharing in the excitement of discovery when his fingers discovered the slick, wet heat of her arousal.

He growled erotic words of praise as he stroked and teased, then his mouth left hers to close over the tip of her breast. She cried out as his teeth and lips pulled at the nipple until it was hard and wet beneath the silk of her blouse. She plucked at the buttons of his shirt, but he just laughed and diverted her with a swift, deep stroke of his fingers.

His mouth switched its attentions to her other nipple, and she arched against the arm that held her close . . . and safe.

She'd never felt so incredibly safe.

Minutes later—or was it longer than that?—she was prone and naked, and wouldn't have realized it were it not for the sudden distraction of cool sheets at her back. She stared up at the man sitting beside her, who was tugging at the knot in his tie with one hand and cupping her breast with the other.

She wondered what sort of magic he practiced.

"Did I faint?" she asked, only half joking. Her fierce response to his touch was stunning, even though his fingers were only lightly caressing her breast.

"You enjoyed," he said, grinning with satisfaction as he lightly pinched the erect nipple he'd been teasing.

She couldn't believe he was still dressed. "I tried," she said in a small voice. It was embarrassing, finding herself nude while he was fully dressed. His tie flew across the room, quickly followed by his suit coat and shirt.

She felt marginally better.

"You tried what?" he asked, indulgent amusement in his expression as he quickly pulled off shoes and socks.

"I tried to undress you."

He smiled. "I know you did, honey. I just knew that if you succeeded, I wouldn't have been able to resist your . . . charms for long." He stood, unzipped his slacks, and shoved those and his shorts down his hips. He watched Sally's face as she got her first look at his arousal, hard and swollen with desire. Her eyes widened just fractionally, and he had to give her credit. She didn't express anything but anticipation.

He wasn't her first man, he knew. But he was the first one in a very long time. He wouldn't have been surprised if she'd revealed a little nervousness.

Sally was more honest than that. She smiled back at him. "Who says I wanted you to resist?"

A hard, masculine knee dented the mattress beside her hip. She waited . . . a little breathless, a lot excited . . . for his reply. He took his time, pushing her legs together so he could straddle them, kneeling above her with his hands free to wander and explore.

He caught her hands as she raised them to do some exploring of her own, tucked them under the pillow at her head—"so that you won't get in my way," he teased—and she asked him again why he was resisting.

He smiled and still didn't answer.

She waited as he touched and then left one breast for the other.

She waited as he drew a line between the small soft mounds to her belly button.

She waited, her breathing a little harsher, her gaze following his, as he continued the line downward until he reached the wet core he'd explored just minutes earlier.

"I guess I let my own desires get ahead of me," he finally said, edging his knees a few inches out and back as he used both hands to relearn her texture. He heard her gasp of pleasure when he slid two fingers into her slippery, hot sheath. "I wanted to get to know you, just a little."

His eyes didn't miss the hard swallow she pushed down her throat. He continued to strike, his rhythm uneven and unexpected, because he wanted to be with her when she turned the corner to ecstasy.

She'd almost turned it alone, just minutes ago when he'd held her in his arms and begun to learn her most erotic secrets. But he'd maintained control, drawing her back when she would have climaxed without him.

Not their first time, he'd decided.

They would do this together.

"I think you know me," she said, ending on a cry as his thumb touched the sensitive bud. Her fingers curled into the soft pillow, and she wished he'd let her touch him back.

She wanted to learn about him too.

Her enjoyment was Hank's delight, and he knew enough about her to believe it would work both ways. Giving in to the desire that was close to driving him insane, he leaned forward until his elbows were all that kept him from crushing her.

Then he lowered himself another inch so that he could feel the tips of her breasts against his chest.

It was better than he'd dared to dream, better still when she ran her hands across his shoulders and began her own exploration.

Her hands swept across his back, his sides, down his arms, quick, light strokes that were followed by a slower investigation. As she opened her mouth to his, Sally luxuriated in strong, firm muscles that rippled under her touch. Her tongue tangled with his, her hips rose and fell in search of him.

He deftly avoided giving in to her silent urgings. She dug her fingernails into his shoulders in a ploy to bring him closer. He laughed into her mouth and schooled patience.

She didn't want to learn that.

"Sally?" he asked softly, his lips sliding across her face and onto her shoulders, which glistened with sweat. She was hot and passionate and so incredibly beautiful in her excitement.

She was exactly what he'd always wanted in a woman.

She just didn't know yet how perfect she was.

"Hmm?" she murmured, her eyes closed now. Not because she didn't want to see, but because the things Hank was making her feel were so wonderfully vibrant. She'd discovered by accident that the intensity of those feelings seemed to increase when she didn't look.

"I've stopped resisting," he said, his mouth moving against hers as he began to take the initial steps that would make things work. She accommodated him when he tried to push one knee between her thighs, liking the way the wiry hair on his legs tantalized hers.

With his hands he spread her further, adding a second knee between her thighs.

She looked up at him, and was suddenly afraid. Not for herself or because of what they were doing. No, Sally wasn't afraid of the conventional things.

She was suddenly, inexplicably, afraid for Hank.

He could feel her fear. It clutched at his heart, and where one moment all he'd wanted was to bury himself deep inside of her, all he could think to do now was give comfort.

He prayed she would take it.

"What is it?" He cupped her face between his hands. "Tell me."

"Everyone thinks I'm mad," she whispered, knowing that it was a totally inappropriate point to bring up at a terribly inappropriate moment. It didn't matter.

Relief nearly overwhelmed him. Unable to help himself, he resorted to teasing. "Not everyone, love. Some people think you're a witch."

She glared at him and stubbornly pursued it. "Either way, doesn't it bother you?"

"No."

"What will people say if they find out you're . . . well, *involved* with Mad Sally? Won't they think you're crazy too?"

He smiled and shook his head. His lips brushed hers, and in whispers interspersed with kisses, he told her to stop talking nonsense.

"Mad Sally can't scare me away. Not now."

She believed him because she wanted to. Melting under the kisses that were steadily becoming less comforting and more provocative, she wrapped her arms around his neck and surrendered in the only way she could.

He drew away an inch or so and held her gaze until he, too, was convinced they wanted the same thing. And then, reaching down with hands that were solid and hard and shaking just a little, he clasped her hips and tilted her slightly as his hard shaft nudged her moist entrance.

Slowly, so there was no mistake that this was an act of love—even though he didn't think she would recognize it as such—he filled her until there was no room for more.

And then, as his body began to move in a slow rhythm, as she helplessly, *wantonly*, joined in that erotic rhythm, he kissed her ever so gently and said, "Sally, love, if this be madness, may it never end."

The yellow-feathered chicken asked if they wanted French fries or onion rings. Sally giggled and said both, unable to take her eyes off the chicken. She'd never been to Ma's Very Own Chicken before.

"Anything to drink?"

Hank checked with Sally, then asked for iced tea. The service person disguised as a chicken totaled their order on the cash register, took Hank's money, and asked for a name he could call when it was ready.

It was the best straight line of the century.

"Mad Sally," she said before Hank could respond.

He scowled ferociously at both her and the gawking chicken before dragging her aside so the next person in line could have a chance at the paltry poultry menu, which was the best he'd been able to do at quarter past midnight in a small town.

He glared at her when she started to laugh as the chicken passed the word and the entire kitchen force came out to stare at Mad Sally. She smiled brightly at the ogling quartet and tucked her hand into the crook of Hank's arm so that he wouldn't try to leave without her.

Several customers turned to stare as well. Sally glanced down at her faded jeans and fisherman's knit sweater and wished she'd brought her cloak along for effect. A couple of people looked disappointed.

Hank had insisted she leave it at home.

She thought that Hank's pretending to be upset with her was a nice touch. It lent credibility to her claim. She plucked a handful of napkins from the dispenser behind him and wondered how long the chicken would take. She was extraordinarily hungry.

Hank was considering whether he should strangle her there or wait until they were alone. He'd never imagined she would do something as foolish as announce her notorious alias to a bunch of fast-food workers.

It occurred to him to be grateful they hadn't gone to Le Casa di Antoine after all.

If he was going to convince the entire population of Oakville that Sally was at least marginally sane, he would need her cooperation. Mad Sally was going to have to go away. Permanently.

Tonight was not a good beginning.

He'd have his own reputation to think about. He led a conservative lifestyle. People *expected* lawyers to act with a certain degree of decorum. There was no margin for witches or madwomen.

Sally Michaels, however, could have all the room she wanted.

He sighed heavily and said, "Doesn't it bother you to know everyone here is staring at you and wondering if you're really Mad Sally?"

"No." She grinned and lifted a hand to straighten his tie. "Does it bother you to talk to a teenager dressed up like a chicken?"

He was saved from answering by a booming "Mad Sally" call over the mike. Sally grasped Hank's arm and pulled him back to the counter, where he handed her the sack of food, grabbed the drinks, and dragged her out to the car.

"How come you didn't want to eat inside?" she asked, balancing dinner on her knees as he pulled out of the parking lot.

"While everyone watched and debated whether or not to call the guys in little white jackets?" he muttered, turning down a residential street. About fifty yards along he pulled over and shut off the engine.

She giggled. "You're overreacting, Hank. Besides, little white jackets went out with Wonder bread and nouvelle cuisine. Now all the psycho specialists wear leather jackets and trainers."

Stopping just shy of asking how she knew that, Hank grabbed the sack of chicken and doled it out. Two for him, three for her. She'd said she was hungry.

He was ready to stuff a drumstick down her throat.

Instead, he took a ferocious bite of a crispy thigh and snagged one of the iced teas. Leather jackets and trainers, he thought. Sally knew more about nut cases and the handling thereof than he was comfortable with.

"Somehow," she said conversationally, "I think eating in your car is something you rarely do. While leather seats are ideally suited for such picnics, I don't picture you as a drive-through patron."

He grunted.

"Anyway, everyone was staring at *me* in there, not you. They won't even remember the color of your eyes after they've told everyone about me." She finished off her first piece of chicken and started in on the next without worrying too much about how he was having trouble coping with Mad Sally's disreputable reputation.

She'd teach him to enjoy it as much as she did.

"Maybe," he said, "I'm stuffy enough not to want to be seen with a crazy lady."

She let that one slide off her back. "Try dressing differently," she suggested. "All those ties must be incredibly inhibiting. Have you ever tried a jogging suit?"

Hank ground his teeth and wondered what it was that had attracted him to Sally in the first place. Then she leaned across the console and kissed him.

Memory returned.

It had been love. Pure and simple.

He wondered what she'd do when he insisted they bury Mad Sally at the earliest opportunity.

Hank walked her to her door but wouldn't go in.

"I've got court again tomorrow," he said between kisses and nuzzles. "It's late."

As much as Sally wanted him to come in, she realized it was for the best. For the time being, until they got better acquainted, she thought it might work to her advantage if Hank wasn't exposed to the "dreadful uglies" of her postsleep persona.

Besides that, she herself had to get back to work. As most of her nights were spent working, she'd already sacrificed a big part of her professional schedule. But then, her boss never made noises until it was time to panic, and none of the manuscripts in her possession were even close to that stage.

Deeply involved in nuzzling a spot just above his collar, she found herself sorely tempted to spend the second half of the night exactly as they'd spent the first. Wrapping her fingers around his tie, she urged him closer until she could trace the curve of his ear with her tongue.

She made all sorts of promises if only he'd cooperate by coming in.

He wouldn't. Covering her mouth with lips that were at once demanding and indulgent, he brought her even closer to the point of trashing any and all plans; then, with regret clear in his expression, he backed away down the sidewalk.

"Have dinner with me tomorrow?" he asked, halfway to the car.

"Think you can get a table at Le Casa di Antoine," she asked, "remembering that you didn't call to cancel tonight?"

He groaned. "I'll probably have to beg, but I'll do my best. Just for you." He backed into the picket gate and nearly fell over it.

Sally laughed and waved him away.

He got into the Jaguar; then, before she had a chance to go inside, he lowered the window and shouted, "Leave Mad Sally at home!"

Nine

Leave Mad Sally at home.

Sally dawdled over her sunrise cup of tea, pondering his parting words. *Leave Mad Sally at home.*

Was he crazy? She shook her head and had to admit that Hank really didn't understand that her shield was now her constant companion.

Mad Sally was as much a part of her life as Raspberry.

"If he'd told me to leave *you* at home, I would have understood," Sally said to the furred creature, whose head was buried in a bowl of lettuce. "After all, Raspberry, I have to believe you'd like fancy restaurants about as much as fancy restaurants would like you. Unless, of course, we're talking menu items here, in which case they'd probably think you're one primo rabbit."

Raspberry repositioned his bulk so that the center of the bowl was precisely under his nose and his tail was turned toward Sally. She got the message and quit razzing him.

Idly leafing through the manuscript she'd just finished editing, she yawned and thought about going to bed for a couple of hours. She checked her watch and figured she had twelve hours before Hank picked her up for dinner. She could sleep a little, then maybe call Annette in New York to let her know she'd send the manuscript overnight that afternoon.

So what was she going to do with the rest of her day? She debated the merits of a long afternoon nap versus a quick trip to Fairview to pick up some groceries, and finally decided not to decide until after lunch. She had other things on her mind that kept her from getting bogged down with insignificant details.

Things like Hank. And Mad Sally.

Leave Mad Sally at home? Simply impossible.

She got up from the kitchen table and dumped the dregs of her tea into the sink. "Maybe Hank just needs to get to know Mad Sally a little better," she said thoughtfully. "Perhaps then he'll appreciate her . . . versatility."

Suddenly, an extremely daring course of action found its way through the maze of her thoughts. She grinned into the early morning sun as she turned the idea over in her mind.

The idea became a plan.

A furry body edged its way across her bare feet as Sally stood at the sink and plotted. She wiggled her toes but otherwise didn't bother the almost slumbering rabbit. Raspberry loved sleeping on her feet.

"Do you know something, Raspberry?" she asked softly.

Raspberry's whiskers brushed her ankles, but he otherwise didn't appear interested. She stared down at the rabbit and told him anyway.

"I think that today Mad Sally will introduce herself to the legal circles of Oakville."

Raspberry grunted and fell fast asleep.

She shrugged off his lack of enthusiasm and reached up to tickle a shiny new leaf on the philodendron hanging beside the window. After sliding her feet from beneath the unconscious rabbit, she picked up the manuscript and went into her office in search of a mailing envelope.

With a smile of mischievous anticipation on her face, she addressed the package and murmured, "*Caveat legistor*," which was the closest her high school Latin could come to coining the phrase "let the lawyer beware."

"So when my client, Jason Powell, made arrangements to donate his house and property to be used as a camp for inner-city teenagers, you began to wonder if maybe he wasn't in his right mind?" asked Hank, checking his watch as he continued his cross-examination. Four hours before he was to see Sally.

He could hardly wait.

"That's for sure," the witness agreed, shaking his head at the sheer stupidity of such a move. "I mean, it was a prime piece of real estate. Why, I heard that Ed Flanders over at Mountain View Realty had offered Jason half a million for it just last summer."

Hank nodded absently, wondering if he should take flowers when he picked her up, then centered his thoughts on his job. It had never been so difficult before. "What did you have to say to Mr. Powell about that?"

"I told him he was making a mistake," Wilson said. "With the real estate market in this area in such bad shape, I considered that to be a serious financial blunder." He shifted in his chair, crossing his legs.

"Didn't you feel a little more strongly than that?" Hank asked.

Wilson nodded, then acted as though he was reluctant to say the next words. "I told him he was out of his mind to give it away when he could have gotten five hundred thousand dollars for it."

"Out of his mind?"

"Senile," Wilson added, then glanced at the elderly man sitting alone at the long table he shared with

Hank. "He's ninety-two. I told him he doesn't know what he's doing."

Hank looked properly somber and continued. "Did Ed Flanders over at Mountain View Realty ever tell you who was behind that half-million-dollar offer?"

"Objection," the lawyer for Jason Powell's heirs drawled without getting up. "Hearsay evidence and immaterial."

"Sustained," the judge said.

Hank let it go for the moment because he knew who was behind the offer. In fact, he hadn't been looking for an answer at all. He'd just wanted to rattle the witness.

He heard a commotion in the courtroom behind him, but didn't let it distract him. Wilson was fidgeting, and Hank knew he'd hit a nerve. He thought he'd let it twitch a minute or so before he let Wilson off the hook—temporarily. Resting his forearm on the wooden rail of the witness stand, he smiled at the middle-aged man.

"Do you know what Jason Powell's property is worth, Mr. Wilson?" he asked.

Wilson turned bright red, cleared his throat, and coughed a few times into his fist before saying, "No."

Hank shrugged as though he hadn't really cared and clenched his teeth to keep from laughing. "Let me ask something you know, Mr. Wilson. Did you tell my client he was senile the following week when he told you he intended to spend the winter in the Caribbean?"

Wilson's eyes narrowed as he tried to figure out if this was a trick question. Hank let his gaze shift to the wall behind Wilson's shoulder so that he wouldn't be intimidated.

Wilson apparently decided there couldn't be any harm in it. "Yes," he mumbled.

"What was that?" Hank asked. "We couldn't hear you."

"Yes, I did," Bud Wilson said a shade more clearly.

"Told him he was off his rocker when he came over to ask me to pick up his mail for him. I said that in my opinion, a ninety-two-year-old man has no business flitting around the world by himself."

"But you agreed to his request anyway."

Wilson said yes.

"Exactly what did he ask you to do with his mail?"

Wilson frowned. "He wanted me to pick it up—"

"Your mailboxes are together?"

"Yep. Right there at the end of the road. Anyway, he wanted me to give it to my daughter, Ann. You see, she runs a secretarial temp company that has a branch in Oakville, and he wanted to pay her to take care of it for him."

"Why didn't he call her himself?"

"He was in a hurry. Made his plans one night and was up at my house the next morning with this list." Wilson was beginning to relax again. "That was a Sunday, so I guess he figured Ann wouldn't be working."

"Did he explain to you what he wanted done?" Hank asked.

Wilson nodded. "Had to. Ann wasn't there."

Hank smiled. "Will you tell the court what he said?"

The opposing attorney objected, probably out of boredom, Hank thought, but Hank held firm and convinced the judge it was important to his case. The judge didn't necessarily agree, but decided to give him some leeway.

That leeway, Hank knew, would go a long way toward keeping his client out of a rest home and in full possession of the fortune he'd earned drilling for oil in the forties.

Powell's kids wanted the money for themselves. Giving away the property hadn't set too well with the three middle-aged children—two men and a woman. Now that he intended to spend another chunk of his fortune wintering in the Caribbean, the heirs-to-be were downright miffed.

It didn't help matters that they'd had to learn everything from other sources. Jason Powell had confided to Hank that he'd never intended to tell them at all. Considering none of the kids had been to visit in over five years, he didn't figure it was any of their business what he did. Besides, he'd set aside what he considered to be adequate inheritances for all of them.

The kids, apparently, had expectations that surpassed "adequate." Legally, however, their only recourse was this competency hearing. Once they won this, rumor was they intended to get Jason's act of charity revoked. That was after they tucked him away in a convenient home for the aged.

Hank prodded the witness to continue.

"He told me to give my daughter the mail and for her to sort through it. He gave me a list of where everything was supposed to go."

Hank heard someone snicker in the courtroom and was startled to see the judge's quelling gaze dissolve into incredulity. He ignored it.

"Did you read this list?" Hank asked. Wilson nodded. "Give me an example."

"Well, all the official things from the bank were to go to his accountant."

"What else?"

"Bills were to go there too." Wilson went on to detail other categories and where they were to be sent. Anything from a certain firm of lawyers was forwarded to a man in Denver, who was apparently handling the sale of yet more property. Mail from the foundation that was receiving his property was sent to his attorneys, and so on. Hank encouraged Wilson with a nod now and then. It was a boring process, particularly as the list had been incredibly well detailed.

A chuckle that sounded like a cackle brought another sharp glance from the judge, but that was all he did. Glance. There was no reprimand, but instead an odd expression of disbelief. Hank was mildly curious, but he kept his back to the courtroom, even when a ripple of laughter washed over the room. It eluded him how anyone could be amused by Wilson's statement that "personal letters were to be forwarded to where he was staying."

Hank finally interrupted as Wilson got to what Jason Powell had said to do about junk mail. "Why didn't he just ask the post office to forward everything to where he was staying?"

"He said he didn't want to see anything but personal mail. And he was afraid that something might get lost with all that mailing back and forth."

"And his house and property, Mr. Wilson? Did he say what was to be done with it?"

"He said he'd gotten someone to oversee the movers once the escrow closed on the transfer."

"Let me summarize, then, if you don't mind," Hank said, turning slightly so that he faced only the judge. "Jason Powell apparently decided to take a vacation one night, made arrangements for his personal property to be cared for, wrote out a detailed forwarding list for correspondence, booked passage and accommodations, and left town. All within twenty-four hours."

Hank grinned and turned back to the witness. "Is that correct?"

"Yes, sir."

"I have no more questions for this witness, Your Honor," Hank said, satisfied. Now all he had to do was show that Bud Wilson was the man behind the half-million-dollar property offer—and that, in fact, Jason Powell's little corner of real estate had recently been appraised for double that figure. To tie things up, he'd show the court that Wilson, acting out of pique, had contacted the heirs with a deal to purchase the property if they could get the charitable donation revoked.

After Wilson's boringly thorough recitation of Jason's trip preparations, no one but a fool would pronounce Jason Powell incompetent without a deeper investigation of the case. The fact that Jason had spent nearly two weeks "having a ball" in the Caribbean—without getting lost, disoriented, or even swindled—would be added proof that he was merely exercising his right to have fun and dispose of his assets as he saw fit.

The judge, Hank knew, wasn't a fool. Glancing at the notes in his hand, he was about to call his next witness when a cackle again filled the air. He glanced over at the judge, who just looked helpless.

Hank had never seen that particular expression on the judge's face before, so he turned to see what had stymied judicial clout. His gaze landed on a figure in the front row. He recognized the cloak.

He saw the knitting needles being worked with frenzied vigor.

And then she cackled. Again.

Mad Sally impersonating Madame DeFarge. No wonder the judge was incapable of action.

Hank counted to ten before he spoke. "I'd like to request a short recess, Your Honor," he said quietly.

"To do what?" asked the judge, after dragging his gaze from the mind-boggling vision in the front row.

"To do whatever is necessary."

His Honor granted a fifteen-minute recess and banged his gavel. Everyone, including the judge, stayed seated. Madame DeFarge cackled and clacked her knitting needles.

Hank strode across the room and closed his hand around her arm.

The courtroom tittered.

He hauled her to her feet, and the hood fell back.

The courtroom gasped.

Hank gritted his teeth and scowled at her. Sally put aside her knitting, stood on her toes, and kissed his chin.

The courtroom sighed.

Hank pulled her over to a side door, where he asked the bailiff if there wasn't perhaps a cell free. The uniformed man shook his head and offered his office. Hank wanted steel bars and a key, but he settled for what he could get.

He shoved Sally inside the bailiff's office, slammed the door, pushed her onto the sofa, and began to pace. He could take only two strides before hitting a wall. He stared at the wall and wondered if it was plaster or brick, because he wanted to put his fist through something, and the wall was convenient.

He took a deep breath and paced in the other direction, his gaze riveted to the floor.

"You're angry," said Sally, watching him stride furiously as she tried to tune into whatever was bothering him.

"Damn right I'm angry!" he shouted. "Wouldn't you be if someone tried to sabotage your career?"

"What sabotage?" she asked, laughing as she remembered the startled look on the judge's face when she'd started her act. "If you hadn't made a point of showing everyone you knew me, they would have gone home thinking exactly what I intended them to think."

"And that was?" he asked, his voice suddenly quiet and calm—a change that made Sally more than a little nervous. He stopped pacing and stood before her with his hands fisted at his sides.

She decided to bluff her way through. "It was a lark. I wanted everyone to think they'd seen the reincarnation of Madame DeFarge in Oakville. Imagine the stories they'll take home!"

"Madame DeFarge," he repeated.

Oh, dear, she thought. Maybe he hadn't got the joke. Now she was really worried. "You know, Hank. Madame DeFarge? *A Tale of Two Cities*? The French Revolution?"

He didn't say anything. His eyes glinted with barely suppressed anger.

"The old lady who cackled and knit as people were sentenced to the guillotine?" she said, a definite squeak in her voice. She'd made a *major* miscalculation, she berated herself as she slipped her gaze past his before it scorched her. Hank was totally incensed.

He carefully sat down in a chair opposite the couch, never looking away from her.

She gulped and gave it one more try. "Madame DeFarge—the old biddy who sat down by where the heads rolled off after they, well, sliced them off?"

"I know who Madame DeFarge is," he said evenly. "I just don't know how I'm going to convince anyone in this town that you're sane if you keep pulling stunts like this."

"Why should you want to?" she asked, puzzled by this turn of events. She'd never thought past Hank's acceptance of her relative normalcy. Why should he?

"Why indeed," he murmured half under his breath. "Especially when you're doing everything in your power to keep them thinking you're totally mad. And now you've got them wondering about me." He thrust his fingers through his hair and stared at his shoes.

"Get a grip, Counselor." Sally bolted from the sofa and began to pace herself, her cloak swirling at her feet as she crossed the short span of linoleum. She was satisfied to note that she could get three strides and not the meager two Hank had achieved. "If you weren't so stuffy, you'd realize Mad Sally has great potential."

"Potential!" he exploded, bursting out of his chair to halt her pacing. "Mad Sally is one of the most selfish people I've ever met!"

"Selfish!" Sally fumed, and thought about grabbing his necktie and jerking his face to her level so that she wouldn't get a crick in her neck staring up at him. But the memories of the previous night were too potent—her fingers had curled around the silken knot, and she'd tugged his lips to hers.

She had to remind herself that she was royally

furious. "All you care about is what people are going to say when they discover you're sleeping with her!"

"And all you want to do is make sure everyone knows you've got at least two screws loose in the best of circumstances!"

"You don't have to yell," she screamed. "I've got audio-assisted eardrums. I can hear you perfectly."

"Maybe I want to yell!"

"You're stuffy!"

"You're selfish!"

"You're up, Counselor," said the bailiff, sticking his head around the partly open door. "Want me to tell the judge you're delayed?"

Hank stared at the man as though he were from outer space until the words sank in. Taking a deep breath, he told him five minutes. Just five more minutes. The bailiff said, "No problem, Hank," and pulled the door shut once again.

Hank had asked for the time because he needed to apologize. The anger that had surged through him was insignificant compared to the chance he'd just taken. Confronting Sally about something so intrinsic to her life was forcing an issue she wasn't willing to discuss. Mad Sally wasn't at fault here. And until he found out why Sally hid behind the shield of madwoman/witch, he was walking on quicksand even bringing it up.

He was sorry, and wanted her to know that before she walked out of his life.

She got her bid in first, though. "What is it about me that makes you so angry?" she asked softly. "That first night you kissed me, you were seething about something."

He sighed, dropping his hands onto her shoulders. "I'm not angry with you, Sally. Never with you. It's Mad Sally who makes me crazy." Honesty, he thought. He couldn't get away from it.

Sally couldn't think of a good answer to that without pointing out how funny it sounded, so she kept her mouth shut and stared up at him, genuinely curious.

"That night," he went on, "when I watched you dancing under the torches, I thought—I *realized*—you deliberately perpetuated the myth of Mad Sally. I felt like a fool for believing the rumors and stories." His jaw tightened at the admission. "Feeling foolish tends to make a person very angry."

"That's all?" she asked softly.

He shook his head. "You're right about the stuffy part too. Lawyers have a tendency to get that way."

She smiled, nibbling her lip as she realized what that must have cost. She gave back in kind. "I guess I am selfish for wanting to have my fun at your expense. This morning when I conceived the plan, I thought it was brilliant." She sighed and looked helplessly contrite. "I just didn't realize you'd *do* anything about it."

He smiled. "You expected me to ignore you?"

She shook her head slowly, long wisps of her hair catching at the hood that cascaded from her shoulders. "I expected you to *laugh.*"

Ten

"Your five minutes are up, Counselor."

Hank cursed under his breath. "I'll be right there," he barked, kicking the door shut. Cupping Sally's face between his hands, he held her half-puzzled, half-exasperated gaze with his own.

"I don't want to fight with you, love," he said, dropping quick kisses onto her face.

She sighed her pleasure, her eyelashes fluttering closed under the tender assault of his lips. "We're not fighting, Counselor," she said. "We're just getting the rules straight."

"Rules?"

"Rules. They're sort of laws with individual biases. For example," she said, brushing her mouth across his chin, "I've got a rule that says nobody picks my crab apples."

He nodded. He was familiar with that one.

She grinned. "It appears that you have one about how onlookers are expected to dress and behave in the courtroom."

"'Behave' is the operative word there," he said darkly. He wanted to say more, but a loud knocking at the door reminded him that he had no time. He dashed back into the courtroom, only to return seconds later to drag her along after him, her cape flying from her shoulders as they sprinted down the short hallway.

"Go home, Sally," he said as he led her through a courtroom that was still filled with people fascinated by the unexpected celebrity in their midst.

"I want to stay," she pleaded. "I'll behave. I promise."

Ignoring scattered cries of "Let her stay" and "Sit with us, Sally," he shook his head. "I want to *win*, love. Now go away so I can concentrate."

She stole another kiss and waited until she was almost out the door before raising her voice to ask about dinner. By the time the judge intervened with a resounding bang of his gavel, Hank looked as though he might have a headache.

He didn't look any better moments later when she dashed back into the room to retrieve her knitting. He suffered that final intrusion in silence, but the warning in his eyes made her dispense with her plan to slip into a back row on the way out.

The nightmare glided into her unconscious mind with the ease of many years' practice. Snuggled beneath a light blanket, which was all she needed in the still-warm afternoon, Sally mumbled words of protest that were no defense against the recurring dream.

It began at the beginning of the end.

"I'll call the fire department." Sally dropped the tablecloth she'd been folding onto the picnic table and rushed toward the kitchen door.

"Don't be a goose," John said. "I'll have that piddling little fire out before nine-one-one even answers the phone."

She halted midstride and turned to take another look at the flames. John was probably right, she thought uneasily. The "piddling little fire" wasn't really much at all, just a small bush alight at the edge of their property. And her husband was already dragging the hose across the lawn toward the flames.

"Do you think I ought to remind the neighbors that fireworks are illegal in this town?" she shouted, hoping her voice would carry across the fence to where merrymakers were celebrating the Fourth of July in traditional style. That was where the stray rocket had originated—a visual dud on one side of the fence that had turned into a dangerous incendiary on the other.

"I'll take care of that too," John said. "After I put out the fire."

She nodded, her gaze lifting to the stand of aspen some fifty feet beyond the wooden rail fence. She felt a sense of relief that the rocket hadn't landed there. It had been a dry summer to date, and the wild grass and flowers that grew amid the weeds beneath the trees were already brown and drying from lack of rainfall.

Sally threw off the blanket and tossed fitfully against the cushions of the sofa. Deep inside her head, she *knew* it was a dream, but she couldn't make herself wake up. And there was always the thread of hope that it would turn out differently, if she could only break through the rigid parade of details.

She had to try.

"Turn on the water," John shouted, and Sally ran to the faucet at the side of the house. She gave the metal knob a twist and saw the hose stiffen as water rushed into it.

"Turn it on, I said!"

"I did!"

She noticed then that nothing was happening on John's end. He threw down the nozzle and retraced his steps, looking for a kink, she guessed. She did the same from her end, squinting in the almost total blackness of the night. Her gaze lifted for a moment to where the yellow and orange flames were now enthusiastically licking their way across the ground toward a shed where they stored the garden equipment.

The fire was spreading.

Her heart thundered in her chest, and she didn't take another breath until she saw John bend down and grab the hose. "Got it," he shouted, but there was no triumph in his voice.

There was worry.

Her husband raced back to where the flames were threatening the shed. "Call nine-one-one!" he yelled. "It's spreading too fast."

Sally started to whimper. Tossing about, tears staining her cheeks, she transited the dreamscape with sluggish obedience.

She didn't really have a choice.

Sally bolted toward the house. Throwing open the kitchen door, she dodged a chair and made a grab for the telephone, hardly noticing when her foot tipped over the cat's water bowl. With her gaze glued to the scene beyond the window, she made the call for help and ran to the sink.

She reached below and pulled out the bucket she used for mopping the floor. Setting it under the tap, she turned on the water, then shut it off again when she realized John needed all the pressure he could get.

Blankets! She raced to their bedroom and pulled off the quilt. Goose down? Totally use-

less! She threw it aside and grabbed a wool blanket. Running back into the kitchen, she lost her footing and fell hard on her hip. The spilled water from the cat's bowl, she knew in an instant, and struggled clumsily to her feet with the blanket still in her arms.

Her gaze darted to the window, and the scene outside knocked the breath from her lungs. The wall of the shed was a sheet of flames, and she thought she could already see where it had burned a hole in the wood.

The gasoline!

She dropped the blanket and stumbled to the door, shoving it open. She screamed a warning.

John looked over his shoulder at her, and she began to run toward him when he didn't move away. She could see him more clearly as she closed the distance between them, worry drawing harsh lines in his face as he battled the flames. She shouted, "The gas . . . in the shed . . . get out of there befo—"

In that split second Sally's entire world exploded in a deafening roar.

Sally screamed—a loud, high-pitched wail that tore across her vocal chords and wrenched her from the fiery depths of the nightmare.

Awake—thank God!—she grabbed the wicker back of the sofa and pulled herself into a sitting position, trying at the same time to catch her breath. That was always the worst part—the incredible tightening of her lungs as though the smoke were actually suffocating her. Her chest heaved as she fought for each tiny breath. Five years' worth of nightmares, and she could still smell the smoke.

She forced her eyes wide open and swallowed hard. It was over now. At least, this one was over. There would be more of the same, always striking when she least expected. She'd grown to accept that.

The nightmare was why she slept in the day whenever possible, saving the dark hours of night for work. It was an attempt to make the inevitable more palatable. During those first few months after the explosion she'd made the mistake of sleeping at night. The horrible dream was stronger then, harder to push aside upon awakening. It wasn't exactly a snap in the light of day, either, but she had long ago realized that any edge was better than none.

The nightmare would never go away. Sally accepted that. She didn't want it to. It served a purpose as a constant reminder against foolish behavior.

The nightmare was also the fuel that sustained Mad Sally.

She shoved aside the lingering shadows with an unusual show of force. Wandering back through the house to the kitchen, she opened the refrigerator door, pulled out a carton of milk, and carried it over to the counter. Her hands shook a little as she poured out a glass—they always did in those first waking few minutes.

She could put up with the nightmare, she knew, but not with being alone. Not anymore.

It was time to tell him, she decided. Hank and Mad Sally were never going to get along until he understood her better. A breeze from the open window over the sink fluffed the curtains, and Sally held the cold glass to her lips as she enjoyed the cooling respite.

Perhaps then Hank would accept Mad Sally for who she was and Sally Michaels for who she wasn't. And it would reinforce that Sally had only so much to give.

She presumed he'd already set up his own ground rules, most of which matched her own. It didn't make sense to expect otherwise. After all, what would Hank Alton, esteemed counselor and respected member of the community, have in common with Mad Sally?

Nothing. She drained the glass and banged it down on the counter. Checking the clock above the stove, she figured she could get in an hour's work before she had to get ready to go out.

Thinking of the night ahead put a smile back on her face, and she was actually whistling an off-key rendition of "Classical Gas" as she carried a virgin manuscript to the living room for its first-ever read by anyone in the publishing industry.

New authors excited Sally. Discovering a *good* new author was like striking gold—thrilling at first sight and a hell of a lot of work from then on.

She opened her mind and prayed for gold.

Le Casa di Antoine was the hottest ticket in town that night. Those who couldn't get a table crowded along the bar that ran the length of the dining room, working the mirror behind it for a not-quite-discreet glimpse of the woman sitting with Hank Alton.

"This wouldn't have happened if you hadn't asked—in front of the entire courtroom—what time I was picking you up for dinner," Hank grumbled.

"What wouldn't have happened?" Sally flicked her gaze down the elbow-room-only row of bar patrons and raised her eyebrows in question.

Hank exchanged shrugs, one of those totally masculine "I bet she's not going to admit this" shrugs, with the waiter. "All those people staring at us. At you." The waiter traded empty salad plates for entrées, then paused for Hank's slightly distracted nod before moving on to less interesting duties.

Hank had to admit he'd never got better service. It had been touch and go for a while, though, until the staff of Le Casa di Antoine had got over the initial jitters occasioned by serving the legendary Mad Sally.

It had been clear from the moment they arrived that rumors of Sally's courtroom shenanigans had preceded them. The maître d', normally dignified and unflappable, had stumbled over a chair en route to their table. It wouldn't have happened if he'd had his gaze on his path and not on Sally's legs—a difficult maneuver under the circumstances, since he was in the lead. Hank could also detect in the maître d' a slight wariness that was probably due to concern about hexes and incantations, but he disregarded it in favor of the legs theory as the reason for the man's clumsiness.

Hank had been tempted to leave when the busboy had had to be forcibly shoved in the direction of their table. He'd expected to have ice water or bread or both dumped into his lap by hands that were visibly shaking. But Sally had saved the occasion by smiling brilliantly at the boy and asking if she couldn't please have a club soda. The busboy had gulped and retreated, and suddenly a glass of the fizzing water had appeared in front of her, with multiple wedges of both lemon and lime on the side.

Obviously, the staff had decided that anyone who drank plain soda water couldn't be all bad. Her legs were likely a plus too. Added to a sexy laugh and friendly radiance, she had managed to displace any and all anxiety sparked by Mad Sally's reputation. They hadn't been in the restaurant five minutes before a pair of waiters and no less than three busboys were taking turns in trying to second-guess Sally's slightest wish.

Hank suspected she'd put them all under a spell.

Her sparkling light blue eyes shimmered in mischievous delight as she assessed the backs presented to the room by the bar patrons. "I guess I just thought Le Casa di Antoine had a very loyal bar following," she said. "It never occurred to me they were here for my benefit."

"Sure it didn't," he said scoffingly, picking up his fork as he noticed she was already well into her dinner. "Just like you didn't realize everyone in that courtroom was hanging on to your every word when you asked if I'd managed to get us a table here."

"I only wanted to know how to dress," she said innocently. "This outfit would have been a touch out of place if we'd had to make do with Ma's Very Own Chicken."

Hank almost stopped chewing as his gaze drifted over the "outfit" in question. The black wool sheath that hugged her body and ended several inches above her knees perplexed him. It was a simple dress, with its modest V neck, three-quarter sleeves, and crystal buttons that closed at her hip. Her coat—a shocking-pink wool that flowed generously from a high collar to a point just shy of her hem line—was equally stylish but fundamentally conservative in cut.

She'd eased the coat onto the back of her chair, declining with a smile the maître d's offer to hang it for her. Behind the shiny, sun-touched waves of hair that caressed her shoulders, he caught occasional glimpses of enormous earrings of the same shocking pink that framed her shoulders.

He couldn't figure out what it was that made the outfit so outrageously exciting. He took another mouthful of whatever it was he'd ordered and studied the whole picture one more time.

"Now who's staring?" she asked softly.

"Just sit back and enjoy it, because staring is all I can do, considering the number of chaperons present," he said in a low voice.

"I'm devastated," she teased.

"I'll take care of that sassy tongue later too," he said, a promise of erotic payback darkening his eyes.

Sally's breath wedged in her throat as images of vivid sensuality tickled her nerves. Smothering a moan of expectation, she twirled her fork in the pasta and studied tonight's version of Hank's uniform. His suit was light gray, the linen shirt beneath it shell pink. Bold splashes of magenta and rose covered his tie.

For a uniform, it wasn't bad. Not bad at all. She slipped some of the creamy pasta between her lips and decided she could get used to Hank's peculiarly formal manner of dressing as long as he continued to do it so well.

He'd admitted more than once that he was stuffy. She agreed. His clothes were an elegant affirmation of that particular character flaw . . . or was it the other way around?" She wondered if there was a way to find out.

"How is your case going?" she asked, cutting a slice of swordfish with her fork.

"It's over." He took a sip of wine and responded to the silent question in her eyes. "Jason said he'd be on the first plane headed in the general direction of the Caribbean."

"Legally?" From the determination she'd seen on the elderly man's face, Sally wouldn't have been surprised if he'd made a break for it if things went against him in court.

Hank tsked and shook his head. "Of course legally," he said. "Did you think I'd try to circumvent the ruling of the court and smuggle him out of town?"

He'd won. She smiled her pleasure at his victory. "I think, given a choice, you'd have run interference if you thought it was the morally correct thing to do."

Hank chose not to debate the what ifs. "Jason asked me to say good-bye to you. He said he wished his kids had turned out with your sense of humor."

"They were real hard cases," she agreed, ignoring the reference to her courtroom antics. "I hope he cuts them off entirely."

Hank shrugged. "Time will tell." At her urging, he went on to talk about other cases, drawing her a picture of his career as it had grown to become a large part of his life. She was fascinated by the scope of problems various people had laid at his feet, enthralled with his sometimes unconventional approaches to helping them.

When he told her about representing an entire third grade class in a suit against a local garbage company that had been unapproachable about recycling programs, she listened with total absorption. Then there was a case of assault and battery in a nearby town, where he'd represented a juvenile delinquent against the determined forces of the police department.

Eventually, he channeled the conversation to stories of Catherine and Willie, then rode the changing tide as he deftly plucked Sally from her role as listener and made her participate.

"What about your parents, Sally? Are they still alive?"

"They were killed in a boating accident when I was eight." Pushing her empty plate aside, she grasped her wine goblet in her fingers and twirled it, reflecting the light of the candle between them. With her gaze on the wine, Hank was in the background, not really in focus. "My mom's aunt raised me. She died of pneumonia while I was in college."

She paused as the waiter returned to clear the table, and accepted the offer of dessert because it was the line of least resistance. Exchanging wine for coffee, she looked up and found Hank's gaze on her. It was steady and curious and wonderfully comforting. She could tell this man about her life, she knew. The thing that surprised her was that she actually wanted to.

Waiting for dessert, they drank coffee and were mostly quiet, except for polite dinner talk. It must have been the lack of outrageous behavior that sent the curiosity seekers away, she decided, because one moment they were there and the next they were mostly gone. Glancing around as the waiter served the lemon torte, she noticed a bare bar and the sparsity of occupied tables.

"Is there no one else?" Hank asked, unwilling to

drop the thread he'd finally begun to pull. "No cousins? Other family?"

She shook her head, picking at the bittersweet dessert as she spoke. "Except for my husband's parents. But I never really got on with them. I think they moved to Florida a couple of years ago."

Husband. Somehow, he'd never suspected that she'd been married. A lover, yes. But a husband? He needed to know more.

"I didn't realize you were married before."

She took a deep breath and nodded. "I met John in college. We were married right after graduation. He died three years later. I moved to Oakville."

Hank sipped his coffee. "That's it?" he asked curiously. "You married. He died. You left."

Sally met his gently reproving gaze and realized how absurd it all sounded. "I don't talk about him very well," she said, grimacing and pushing her almost untouched dessert aside.

She caught the slight smile that curved Hank's lips. It encouraged her to go on. "It was five years ago. We lived in Vermont."

He nodded. "Did you love him?"

"Yes." Melancholy mixed with regret as she remembered the love they'd shared, the few years of playful adventures and mature planning. They'd wanted kids, but later, when there was more time, more money.

She had been content with John. And loved. She'd never doubted that for one moment.

Hank watched the various emotions play across her face and tried to control the fear that gripped his heart. He'd fallen in love with Sally knowing it wouldn't be easy to convince her of that love.

He'd never imagined he might be competing with a ghost.

"Do you still love him, Sally?"

Somehow, she'd known he would ask. Swallowing

over the lump in her throat that always came when she thought about John, she shook her head.

"I don't love anyone. I can't."

The evening was cool and crisp, and Sally appreciated the warmth of her coat. Hank's arm draped her shoulders, too, as they walked along a path that wound through the park on the far side of town.

She told him then, about the explosion. "I lost a lot of my hearing, all of my hair and eyebrows. But I was all right otherwise. Once I got out of the hospital, I realized that I didn't want to stay in a place where everyone wanted to hold my hand and tell me everything would be okay." She shrugged. "It wouldn't, and I knew that. I came here so I could be alone. It was the only thing that made sense at the time."

Hank guided her past a gnarled root that stuck out into the path and didn't say anything. *I don't love anyone. I can't.* It had thrown him at first, until he realized that he'd expected just that sort of resistance from her.

It didn't change what he felt, nor did it alter his intentions. He loved her. He wanted her to love him back.

Some things in life just couldn't be hurried. Sally had fled to Oakville to heal . . . even though she insisted she'd come there to hide. He wondered how long it would be before she understood the difference.

"I have nightmares about the explosion," she said, breaking into his thoughts.

"Do you ever scream during it?" he asked, suddenly realizing how it had all begun. The scream that triggered Willie's fall. He felt an immense tide of protectiveness wash over him as he finally began to understand the horrifying events that colored her days with despair.

"That's what wakes me up," she said. "How did you know?"

He shrugged. "I guessed." There were some things she didn't need to know. "Are they horrible, love?"

"They're real," she said simply. "And I don't like having them, but they remind me to be strong."

He looked down at the top of her head and asked why.

"Because they remind me what happens when you love someone," she said, the logic an undisputed fact as far as she was concerned. "I loved my parents. They died. Then my aunt. And finally, there was John. They're all gone now, all the people I loved. When I was recovering from the explosion, I realized that if I didn't love someone, I wouldn't have to go through the pain of losing them."

"One does not necessarily follow the other," he murmured, urging her to a nearby park bench. He kept her under his arm as they settled beneath the light of a single street lamp. "Loving does not always lead to losing."

She looked up at him with the hard-earned knowledge of experience in her expression. "I've lost three for three, Counselor," she said softly. "I'm not willing to give it another try."

"Aren't you afraid I might be falling in love with you?" he asked.

She shook her head and surprised him with a teasing grin. "You're too stuffy to fall in love with Mad Sally."

"But you let me make love to you." He wondered if Sally was aware of the healing process at all, and how far along she was in it. Couldn't she see that her joking response hadn't really answered his question?

"*With* me," she corrected him provocatively, her face a curious blend of shadows and light that emphasized her clear, bright eyes. "Besides, I wouldn't be here if I imagined there was a chance you would fall in love." Shifting an inch or so sideways, she lifted her face until his shadowed gaze met her own. "I'm trusting you not to do anything stupid, Hank."

She meant "fall in love." He nodded, because he had no intention of doing anything stupid.

He'd already done it.

Eleven

"Aren't you afraid that *you* might fall in love with *me*?" Hank asked.

Sally swallowed hard. "I can't. I won't." Giving him a smile that was almost apologetic, she continued. "It's taken me five years to get strong enough for you, Hank Alton," she said seriously. "I have to believe that I can be with you without falling in love."

"But what if you do?"

"I won't."

He soothed her with a gentle hug and wisely didn't argue. He had to believe that she was talking with her head and not with her heart. How long would it be, he wondered, before he could make her do just the opposite?

A man with a large, furry dog on a leash ambled past their bench, and together they watched his progress until he reached the far side of the park. Sally leaned into the curve of Hank's shoulder, incredibly relieved that he understood. At least, she thought it was relief that brought tears to her eyes. Surreptitiously, she flicked away the errant drops and hoped he wouldn't notice.

She'd have to lie, then, and tell him she always

cried when talking about John. She didn't want to lie to Hank.

"Did I ever tell you how Mad Sally got her start?" she asked, suddenly desperate to get onto another subject.

"You know you didn't."

She rested her cheek on his chest, riding the even cadence of his breathing as his hand made long strokes down her arm, silent encouragement in case she needed it. She didn't, but she absorbed his caress with pleasure. The saga of Mad Sally was laughable and not at all traumatic.

"I arrived in Oakville in early fall. I hadn't been here but a couple of days, when I looked out the window and saw a child in my tree. It was a boy, about the same age as Willie, and I was afraid he'd fall and hurt himself. Anyway, I pulled on the cloak and ran—"

"Why the cloak?" he interrupted.

"My hair," she said, smiling wryly. "Better stated, the lack of it. It was just beginning to grow back then, like my eyebrows. I wore the cloak and hood when I went out to keep people from staring. On the day I saw that kid, it was already reflex."

"So instead of saving the kid from falling, you scared him half to death." Such a simple explanation, he mused.

She nodded and sighed. "It was pretty much like what happened with Willie, except the kid didn't actually fall out of the tree."

"I can buy that part of your story," he said, "but what about all the rumors I heard about you talking to plants and rocks and such? Did someone make those up?"

She laughed. "That had nothing to do with Mad Sally at all. Not in the beginning anyway. I just discovered that with very few exceptions—things like talking to my boss on the telephone and shopping in Fairview—my voice was getting kind of creaky."

"Creaky?"

She nodded. "It was embarrassing to open my mouth and sound like old stairs. I finally decided that I had to exercise my voice a little each day. Talking to myself seemed a batty—"

His chuckle earned him a swift dig in the ribs. "Anyway," she continued, "I started talking to things. Like plants. Everyone knows plants like being spoken to."

"But rocks, Sally?" he chided, skipping the plant justification because his mother frequently chatted at length with the various pots of greenery in and around the house.

"That was for the benefit of my audience," she admitted. "Especially during those first few months, kids lurked all around the wall, waiting for me to do something weird." She shrugged lightly. "I tried to oblige."

"And so it began." His voice rumbled deep in his chest, and she rubbed her ear against the vibration. "The kids discovered Mad Sally had moved into Oakville, and you discovered that Mad Sally was a brilliant way to keep everyone away."

"Once I got the hang of it, it was good entertainment."

"How did you find out they called you Mad Sally if you didn't talk to anyone in Oakville?"

"Spray paint."

He grimaced. "What else have they done to you over the years?" Urging her to her feet, he turned and headed back to the car.

"Nothing exceptional. Just the usual kid stuff. They toss rotten eggs once in a while."

"What else?"

"Besides throwing toilet paper all over the flowers and trees?" She shrugged as though these minor acts of annoyance weren't in the least bit important. "Well, last year someone spray-painted Raspberry's maze. Almost killed it. And on Halloween they set off a stink bomb in my mailbox. The postman couldn't get near it for weeks. Had to leave my mail on the sidewalk."

"Wouldn't bring it to the door?"

"Not on his life." She grinned as he helped her into the car. "I don't think his contract covers Mad Sally."

"I promised Willie he could stay up until I got home," Hank said. "Do you mind if we swing by there?"

Sally shook her head wordlessly because her mind was skipping ahead to when he would take her home . . . and come inside to share with her the long hours of the night. That he would stay was implicit in the words he'd just spoken.

"You think bringing Mad Sally home with you will make him sleep?" she asked.

"I think that Mad Sally has caused enough mischief today," he said darkly. "Besides, Willie thinks you're gorgeous."

"That's not the impression I got."

Hank surprised her by disagreeing. "He's fast becoming your biggest champion," he said. "Ever since I told him about Raspberry's birthday party and the maze, he seems to have decided you're fresh."

"Fresh?"

He flashed her a grin. "Fresh as in cool. Neat."

"Modern slang seems to have passed me by," she said, laughing at the odd expression. "What is it about Raspberry that makes me cool? Or even fresh?"

Hank just shrugged. Explaining to Sally that her eccentric habits were simply that—eccentric—was more of a challenge than he wanted to attempt. He pulled into the driveway of the Victorian farmhouse and helped her out of the car.

"What a terrific house!" she hurried along the walk so she could get a better look. "Does the veranda go all the way around?"

"Just three sides," he said, pleased that she so obviously liked it. It was a hurdle he hadn't considered until that moment. There simply wasn't room for all of them in the house on Blossom Lane.

The fear that he'd fail to win her love nearly brought his heart to a shuddering stop before he managed to control it. He would succeed, he told himself. He had to. He loved her too much to lose this, the most important fight of his life.

He took a deep breath and continued to answer her questions as he guided her inside the house. No, it hadn't been in such terrific shape when he'd bought it. Yes, he and Willie were doing a lot of the work, but he contracted out the bigger jobs. No, the two-storied barn out back wasn't used for anything at the moment, but he had plans to convert part of it into a guest house for Catherine someday.

Sally was asking about the chandelier in the dining room, whether it was the original fixture, when Catherine pushed through the kitchen doors. She smiled when she saw Hank was not alone.

"I heard all about your Madame DeFarge stunt," she said, reaching out to take Sally's hand in hers. "Bill called and said it was the funniest thing he'd ever seen."

"He was apoplectic," Hank said.

Catherine shot her son a pitying look. "*You* were apoplectic. Everyone else thought it was a hoot!"

"Who's Bill?" Sally asked, grinning at the older woman. She was thoroughly delighted to find someone with a sense of humor.

"Judge Stirm," Catherine explained. "Just plain Bill when he's not wearing that black robe."

"Does that mean you're just plain Sally when you're not wearing your robe?" another voice asked curiously.

The three adults turned in surprise to find Willie hovering uncertainly at the bottom of the stairs. Barefoot and dressed in pajamas, he looked pretty wide awake for someone who was supposed to be ready for bed. Hank tugged gently on Sally's hand, urging her to follow as he crossed the wide hallway. A slight sound had Sally looking back over her shoulder to see Catherine disappearing behind the kitchen doors.

"It's not Sally," Hank said in a stern voice once they'd reached Willie. "Mrs. Michaels to you, young man."

"Stuffy, stuffy," said Sally, earning herself a scowl from Hank and a quick grin from Willie. "How can Willie and I be friends if he has to call me Mrs. Michaels?"

"It's proper."

"So are chaperons, but I don't see you demanding one of those," she countered, smiling slyly.

"You need a chaperon?" Willie asked. "I've got some free time tomorro—"

Hank clapped a hand over his son's mouth and looked as if he wanted to do the same to Sally. Giggling beneath the muzzle, Willie watched as Sally sidestepped Hank's halfhearted attempt to do just that. Man and boy tussled for a few moments as Sally rooted for Willie from the sidelines.

When order was finally restored, with Hank and Willie sprawled on the carpeted staircase, Sally suggested that Willie call her whatever he liked.

"Anything except Mad Sally," said Hank, ungraciously surrendering his stand on the Mrs. Michaels issue. Holding out his hand, he urged Sally to join them on the stairs.

She accepted, something indefinable making her want to be part of the scene. Hank's fingers curled around hers as she settled beside him on the stairs.

"I wouldn't call her Mad Sally, Dad," Willie said indignantly. "Only a fool would do that."

Sally captured Willie's gaze with her own. "It isn't anyone's fault but my own what people call me," she said softly.

"Dad says you wanted everyone to think you were crazy."

She smiled at the boy's puzzled expression—it reminded her so much of his father—and proceeded to set the record straight . . . for the second time that evening. "I wanted people to leave me alone," she said. "Pretending to be crazy was a simple way to accomplish that."

Willie nodded sagely. "I understand that part. But I don't understand what you're doing here now if you want to be alone."

Sally sighed and wondered how kids always knew to ask the tough questions. "I'm here because the day you and your dad came to visit me, I realized that I was lonely."

"You didn't know that before?"

"Perhaps I did," she said slowly. "But until that day, I never admitted it."

Willie smiled, and she answered him with a smile of her own. "I'm glad," he said simply. Stealing a look at his father, he added, "Dad needs your kind of woman around."

Your kind of woman. Hank was mulling over Willie's choice of words as Sally asked, "What kind of woman is that?"

"The kind that can tell him to get stuffed and get away with it."

"I told him he was stuffy," she said with a delighted laugh, "not to get stuffed."

"Same thing," Willie said.

Sally spared a glance for the stuffee in question, and discovered to her surprise that he didn't look at all perturbed by the character assassination in progress. Perhaps he wasn't so stuffy after all, she mused.

"What makes you think she gets away with anything at all?" Hank asked, joy filling him as he watched his son and Sally lay the groundwork for a friendship that was, in his view, inevitable.

"She called you stuffy not five minutes ago."

Hank shrugged. "There was a witness. If I did her bodily harm, you'd tell on me. I'd get caught."

"No good, Dad. Half of Oakville heard about what she did in court, and you still took her out to dinner," Willie said logically. "Sounds to me like she got away with it."

Sally smiled sweetly at father and son and said, "Appears to me there are two lawyers on these-here stairs."

Hank muttered something about bedtime and gave Willie a one-second head start before scrambling up the stairs after him. They disappeared amid laughter and frantic shouts. Sally was just dusting off her skirt when Willie reappeared at the top of the stairs.

"Will you come to soccer practice tomorrow?" he asked, looking anxiously over his shoulder for pursuit.

Sally didn't have to think twice. "Does your dad wear a tie to practice?" she asked.

Willie nodded reluctantly.

She grinned. "I'll come anyway."

"I'm sorry about this morning."

Hank spent a long moment nuzzling her temple before answering. "When was this morning?"

Sally swatted his bare butt, then soothed the nonexistent pain with a gentle stroking that made him rethink his impending departure.

"I'm trying to apologize, Hank," she said as his lips moved in slow determination toward her mouth. "The least you can do is pay attention."

"Oh, I'm paying attention, love." Sliding a hand to the moist nest of dark, springy curls between her thighs, he stroked her gently. "I'm paying attention to how excited you get when I touch you here."

Sally arched her back as his caress reawakened desires she'd thought were long since satisfied. She must have been wrong, though, because her hips were nudging against his hand, her breasts swelling and peaking against the rough strength of his chest.

She had something to say. Gulping back a moan of sheer pleasure, she tried very hard to get it out. "You told me I was selfish. I want you to know you're right."

He teased the corner of her mouth with his tongue, laughing softly as she tried to entice him inside. "Selfish is a matter of perspective," he said against her lips. "For instance, this morning I was referring to the distinct possibility that Mad Sally's escapade would distract me from doing the best job I could for my client. I thought you were selfishly entertaining yourself at another's expense."

Sally felt totally chastised. Hank eased the burden of her guilt with gentle kisses on her lips and by dragging his tongue across her teeth in slow torment. Her murmured apologies were swept away by his heated seduction.

Rolling to his back, he kept her anchored firmly against him so that she lay atop the long length of his body. Catching her hips in his hands, he gently forced entry into the part of her that was slick and moist with desire. "On the other hand," he said, his voice low and dark, "there's a kind of selfishness of which you are incapable."

Bracing her hands on his shoulders, she raised herself until their bodies met at only one crucial point. "What kind is that, Counselor?" she asked unsteadily as he guided her in a slow, easy rhythm.

"This." He lifted a hand and made a single stroke from her moist center to the curve of her chin. "For someone who never wants to get close to people, you give a hell of a lot of yourself to me every time we make love."

Sally knew there was something wrong with what he was saying, but she couldn't figure it out. In the next moment, though, it no longer mattered, because Hank drew her inexorably along as he forged a sensually intoxicating pathway to the stars and held her tightly as she absorbed their brilliance.

Panting, quivering, she fell into his arms and shared murmured words of joy. It was over, for now, the love that they made without loving.

Much later, in the uncertain hours that were neither day nor night, he went back to the home where he lived with his mother and son. Sally watched the lights of his car disappear down Blossom Lane and wondered at the impulse that made her want to follow.

Willie played with Raspberry while Sally told Hank about the sack.

"It's something casual," she said, pressing it into his hands and pushing him toward the bedroom door. "I found it this morning in Fairview. You'll love it."

The look on his face said that if it wasn't a tie, he didn't want to know. "I look fine," he said.

"You look terrific," she agreed. "Stuffy, but terrific."

"There's nothing wrong with stuffy." He scowled and held his ground.

"Wear it for Willie," she cajoled. "You intimidate all his friends with that tie of yours."

"I have more than one tie," he said loftily, but sighed his acquiescence and went reluctantly into the bedroom.

Sally winked at Willie and asked if he'd brought the trainers. He darted out the door and returned in a flash with the athletic shoes he'd sneaked from his father's closet. That was the result of the first surreptitious phone call she'd made that morning. The second had been Catherine to discover if she had a camera.

"What do you want a camera for?" Catherine had asked.

"Do you or do you not want a picture of your son in an incredibly sexy exercise outfit?" Sally had asked.

"I do." Catherine had quickly agreed to let Willie transport said camera with the trainers.

"You sure he won't get mad?" Willie asked as words unbecoming a man of the law, so to speak, reached their ears from beyond the closed door.

"Would you rather lose this battle to a silk tie?" Sally asked.

Willie shook his head vigorously just as the bedroom door was shoved open. Hank emerged, sexily resplendent in loose trousers and jacket of pale lilac with black sleeves and trim.

Willie gasped.

Sally gasped . . . and grinned.

Hank gritted his teeth. "This is ridiculous!"

"It's sensational," said Sally, grabbing his hand before he could retreat and retrench. "Mind-boggling, in fact. I never imagined you'd look quite so—"

"Stupid?" he asked dryly.

"Superb," she said, waggling her eyebrows in lascivious approval.

Hank speared his son with a stare that could have wilted jasmine. "Nothing to say, Willie?"

Willie sighed and beamed. "It's totally fresh, Dad. The guys are never going to believe this."

Sally shot Hank an "I told you so" glance and said, "Any other questions?"

Hank nodded curtly. "Can I borrow your cloak?"

Twelve

Hank was a sensation at soccer practice.

Coach and just about everyone else there made it a point to tell him he was a regular fashion plate. Sally laughed and told him to quit grousing and pay attention to how terrific Willie was at running the ball down the field. He needed practice, though, she said, when he got close to the goal. The trick was to keep the goalie in mind without letting him distract you.

Hank asked how she knew so much about soccer. She told him she was a recluse with cable TV.

They went along with the team for pizza after practice, and only one small boy had the nerve to ask if Sally was really the one who lived on Blossom Lane.

When she said yes, he asked if that meant they could have her apples—seeing she was there with Willie's dad and all.

She said that if they wanted to trade fruit from their own gardens for crab apples, she'd be pleased to make the exchange. Then Willie explained what she did with the apples, and soon she had volunteers lining up to help her do everything from gather fruit to make jelly.

How do you make jelly? was the next question.

Hank allowed ten more minutes before dragging her away. It wasn't easy, particularly as Sally had discovered a budding author in Coach.

She promised to read whatever he wrote—a rash promise that was easy to make, given the circumstances. Hank had already told her Coach regularly published articles in the weekly local paper as well as several national magazines, and was only now finding enough time to work on something more complicated.

Gold was where you found it.

Willie made Sally promise she'd show up for his band concert the next evening before he allowed himself to be reabsorbed in the pizza-crazy crowd of kids.

And that was only the beginning.

Hank gave Sally enough time to work and almost enough time to sleep, his schedule melding with hers until empty hours were at a premium. She found herself involved in every facet of his life and enjoying each moment of her newfound freedom. It was a comfort to know she was strong enough to resist getting too close to him, she constantly reminded herself. There was a shield between her and everyone else, a barrier that not even Hank tried to penetrate.

She thanked him for his understanding and threw herself into a whirlwind of activities when he didn't try to argue that she might be wrong. She said yes to everything.

He called and asked her to a concert in the park. She brought a picnic that fine autumn afternoon and insisted Willie and Catherine join them. Another day, Catherine dragged her to her garden-club meeting, and Sally found herself enjoying the variety of people who had gathered to talk about hothouse cymbidiums and frostbitten geraniums. She offered up her own experience as counsel when a gray-haired lady complained that her African violets wouldn't bloom. When she added that talking to them seemed to help, everyone in the room just nodded and asked if she'd got around to naming her favorites.

Hank and Willie went with her to the soup kitchen and made quite an impression on Mort Campbell as they worked together to repair a few of the long tables and benches that had been getting wobbly. Mort's wife, Muriel, was right in the middle of it all, tossing out instructions as quickly as she hammered home the two-penny nails someone had donated for the project. Sally kept busy setting up the soup line for lunch.

Everyone helped serve when the doors opened, and then during the kitchen duty that followed. When it was time to go, Willie marched over to the director and asked if he could bring a couple of friends to help the next time, apologizing that it could only be on weekends and only when they could get a ride.

Hank said he thought he'd be able to bring them when they wanted to come, and Sally felt a pulse of pride in the boy who was growing into the image of his father.

The days grew shorter, autumn leaves colored and fell. Mad Sally was absorbed into the community as though there had never been any question of her sanity. Children who had run in fear now knocked on her door and begged to play with her rabbit. After several weeks of this Sally was thrilled to notice that Raspberry had begun to lose weight from all the exercise he was getting.

Adults who had heard all the rumors now professed never to have believed a single one. The mailman rang her gong and personally handed her the mail on days when it was nice and he could afford the time. Girl Scouts discovered she was an easy target, and Sally was nearly buried under a deluge of cookies.

The Avon lady hung a brochure on her door.

Sally learned to put in her hearing aids first thing in the morning and found she was much too busy to talk to rocks. She still slept as little as possible at night, napping during the day and dealing with nightmares. All in a day's work.

For the first time in five years Sally was happy. There were odd times, hours when she was alone, when she'd suddenly think of John and the joy they'd shared. But the nightmare was a cruel reminder of the past—bad enough in her sleep, even worse when she was awake.

She pushed aside the memories so that the pain wouldn't consume her.

Hank never spent the night with her. He always wanted to be at home when Willie awakened, and Sally agreed. They made love passionately and frequently, and never the same way twice. Hank was boldly sensual in his approach to sex and demanded equal enthusiasm from Sally. She complied with what he said was "indecent fervor," but there was laughter and pride in his voice when he told her he'd never experienced such wanton responsiveness from a woman.

He loved it.

One night they made love without her hearing aids. Sally discovered a new level of sensuality that she wanted to share with Hank, so she stuffed his ears with cotton and let him experience it for himself.

The line between lust and laughter blurred as they basked in new levels of pleasure. Sally had never felt quite so happy as she did in his arms, so excited about life as she did when they were together. And they were together almost constantly. Ordinary chores and everyday living took on a new meaning now that she shared so many of them with Hank.

It made her nervous to think about the way he was gradually becoming a necessary part of her life, so she didn't. Sally had *lots* of practice not thinking about things.

Football and soccer occupied the increasingly cool late afternoons and evenings, Hank and Sally cheering on Willie and his teammates while Hank—albeit reluctantly—bedazzled the crowds on the bleachers with the eye-popping assortment of casual clothes that Sally pressed on him. He argued and resisted and always gave in each time she presented him with something new because he wanted to please her.

In a moment of weakness one night Hank did allow that the clothes were comfortable.

Once, frazzled by the day's events, they fell asleep in the early evening, not even making love before exhaustion overtook them. Hank awoke first, and began to laugh softly as he studied the half-asleep woman beside him. "Is this what you mean by fulfilling my worst expectations?" he asked, studying the fuzzy, misguided hair, crisscross wrinkles, and pink-rimmed eyes.

Sally grunted and told him to shut his eyes and pretend she was a princess.

"Definitely not a witch," he murmured, dragging her those last few steps toward wakefulness and convincing her that he hadn't really noticed anything at all.

Once, at the end of the day, he told her how much better his life was now that he'd met her. Mad Sally cackled raucously and attacked his body.

For the most part, though, Sally took great pains to behave herself—as Hank would describe it. She almost never wore her cloak around Oakville. Only occasionally did she revert to a blatantly Mad Sally escapade. She got caught twice.

She figured it was a good score for someone who was only semireformed.

"How did you get permission to stay out all night?" she asked, snuggling into the warm, naked body lying beside her.

Hank smiled into the darkness. It was the first mention she'd made of the overnight case he'd carried inside about three hours earlier. "I have to spend tomorrow night in Denver," he said, running his fingers across the smooth, moist skin of her back, gently toying with the slight ridges of her spine. "Catherine suggested I might as well take two nights."

Sally giggled against his chest. "Catherine is a very kind woman."

"I think she's tired of hearing me steal up to my room in the middle of the night," he said wryly. "The wood floors in that house creak at the most inconvenient places."

"Maybe you should get the floor fixed," she suggested, stretching like a cat beneath his stroking hand. She almost felt as though she could sleep now, with Hank beside her to keep away the dragons of the night. It would be so wonderful to sleep through the night without fears of waking up alone and afraid.

She yawned and nestled closer.

"It would be easier to move you in with me," he said, as though it were the only reasonable thing to do.

She laughed, already half-asleep. "Yeah, right. I can just see you explain that one to Willie. 'Oh, by the way, Son. I've brought my lover home to live with us.'"

"If you were my wife, there wouldn't be anything to explain."

Sally was instantly wide awake. "Don't even joke about it, Hank," she said testily, drawing away from him until they were no longer touching. "You know how I feel about that."

He reached out and flicked on the bedside lamp. She met his steady gaze with an angry one. "I'm not joking, Sally," he said. "I want to marry you."

She edged backward until there was nowhere else to go. Curling her fingers into the blankets that had fallen around her, she tried hard to fend off panic. With a gesture that was purely defensive she snagged her robe from the foot of the bed and pulled it on.

"Why, Hank?" she demanded.

He shrugged. "I fell in love. . . ."

"I told you not to!" she exclaimed, real frustration coloring her words.

He just smiled, the expression in his eyes entreating her to understand. "It was too late then. It's too late now."

Hugging her arms around her waist, she stared numbly at the man who had turned her life inside out in such a short time. It had been weeks since they'd met, yet he'd brought her out of the complacency of her solitary existence and had made her part of a full, exciting life that . . . She sniffled and shook her head as if she could deny the inevitable. Without Hank, the life he'd shown her would be empty.

Emptier than any loneliness she'd ever experienced.

But she had no choice. Things had gone too far. Emotions she'd thought were tamed were now raging out of control.

He loved her, and he wanted her to love him.

With a quiver of apprehension she knew that she did.

"Tell me you don't love me, Sally," he said, breaking into her thoughts. "I don't think you can. I can't believe that what we share together—"

"You're talking about sex," she said coldly. "You don't have to be in love for that to be good."

He threw off the covers and surged across the bed, grabbing her arms. "I'm talking about *us*—in and out of bed. We're good together, you and me. We laugh and play and work, and it all feels like a holiday because we're doing as much as we can together and sharing what we can of the rest. We argue and make up, and then do it all over again because we disagree about so many things."

His voice deepened, and she listened with growing distress. "Even the arguments are good, Sally, because there's life there. Someone on the other side to share things with. I've seen you grin and pick an argument just for the hell of it . . . or just because you want to make sure I'm there to take the other side."

She swallowed over the lump in her throat and chewed on her lip as he kept on. "There's love in your eyes when you smile at me, whether we're watching Willie play soccer or we're just watching the stars."

A heaviness settled in her heart that she knew would never go away. Love weighted down by the terror of what the future might bring was a ponderous burden, one that she'd tried so hard to avoid.

He shook her when she didn't respond, not ungently but still hard enough to get her attention. "Tell me you don't love me, Sally," he demanded.

"I can't," she said softly. "I do love you."

There was guarded relief in his expression as he said, "Then why does it feel like we have a problem here, love?"

She shrugged his hands away and slipped off the bed. "One thing does not necessarily lead to the other, Hank," she said matter-of-factly as she walked around to the other side of the bed, putting its width between them. Clenching her hands, she tried to prepare herself for the pain she was about to give . . . not even considering what it would cost her in the lonely hours of the night. It would be better this way. A quick, brief slice of heartache versus years of grief.

"I will not marry you. I will not move into your home. Ever."

He was stunned. "Why? We're in love. We should be together."

"That's the difference between us, Counselor," she said harshly. "You want the happy-ever-after. Trust me, it won't happen."

"What are you talking about?"

"I love you, Hank, but I won't go through life being constantly terrified that something will happen to you. *I can't live through that again.*"

"You mean you *won't* live through that again."

Their gazes locked and anger reverberated between them as he challenged her denial and she held fast. Sally knew the precise moment when he believed her.

She nodded almost imperceptibly. "I won't watch you die, Hank. I love you too much for that."

"You'd prefer to go through life without me at all?"

"Yes!"

"Even though I'll probably live to be ninety or a hundred!" he shouted. When she didn't respond, he shouted even louder. *"Dammit, woman! Do you realize how absurd that sounds?"*

"Yes!" she wailed. "Now please just go away and let me get on with my life." Her breaking point wasn't very far away. She could feel the fissure prying open her heart. Oh, God, she prayed. Please keep me sane when he's gone.

"No!" he thundered.

"Can you promise me I won't lose you before we have a chance to grow old together?"

"You know I can't."

"Then this discussion is over." Picking up his clothes that were strewn upon the floor at her feet, she tossed them across the bed to him.

"We're not finished here," he said, ignoring the clothes.

She couldn't take any more. "Yes, we are," she said firmly and plucked the hearing aids from her ears. Hank opened his mouth and shouted at her, but she ignored him and fled into the bathroom, locking the door behind her.

Not long after that, as she sat huddled on the cold tiles, she felt the slam of the front door as Hank walked out of her life.

New tears slipped down already wet cheeks as Sally

shuddered, the silence of the night closing in around her.

Hank knew the pain of living without her within the first few hours after he'd stormed out of her house. He refused to go through that for a lifetime. Even though he wasn't convinced he could help her get over her deep-seated fear of losing those she loved, he had to try.

Sally was his life.

He called her from Denver every chance he got. No answer. Two days passed before the case he was trying was finished. He drove straight to the house at the end of Blossom Lane.

She was gone. Her car wasn't in the shed, and the house was locked up tight. He found the key she kept under a garden rock and let himself in. Five minutes later he knew she didn't plan on returning anytime soon.

Raspberry was nowhere to be found.

He drove to Fairview and tracked down Mort Campbell, who was eating lunch in a café not far from the bank.

"I haven't seen her, Hank," said Mort, wiping mustard from his mouth as he stared up at the unsmiling man beside his table. "You think she might have gone up to the soup kitchen?"

Hank shook his head. "Her rabbit is gone. What's the name of the vet she uses?"

Mort gave him the name and asked him to join him for lunch.

"Thanks, Mort," Hank said. "I'm not in the mood."

Mort nodded. "I guess if Muriel ran away, I wouldn't have any appetite either."

"How do you know Sally ran away?"

"You're looking for her. I just figured she took off without telling you . . . ran away."

Hank swallowed and waited to see if Mort knew anything he didn't.

"Muriel always thought Sally was running from something." Mort put down his sandwich and sighed. "Sally might have fooled a lot of folks with that crazy act in Oakville—"

"You knew about that?"

"Yeah, but we didn't let on. Sally had her own way of doing things, and they were good things, so we never let that Mad Sally routine of hers make a difference." Mort chewed another bite thoughtfully. "Anyway, as I was saying, my Muriel always thought Sally was running from something. If you're looking for her, it appears she's done it again."

Hank nodded and gritted his teeth against the pain that welled up inside him. He'd pushed her too hard, too fast. It was his own fault she was gone, because he'd been too concerned with what he wanted from her and not what she needed from him.

She had only wanted peace, and he'd given her hell. After shaking Mort's hand, Hank left the café and drove to the vet where Sally boarded Raspberry.

The vet wasn't encouraging. Sally had left Raspberry for an indefinite stay. She'd left a number where she could be reached in New York.

Hank didn't take it. He would wait. It was up to Sally to decide if she could take the risk. All the messages on her telephone answering machine would tell her what he wanted her to know when . . . *if* she returned.

He had to believe she'd come back to him. Anything else was unacceptable.

Sally was on her way to New York almost before the tears had dried. A long-overdue trip, she tried to convince herself. Her boss had been asking her to come for a month.

She'd been procrastinating because she hadn't wanted to leave Hank.

She checked into the same hotel she normally frequented, took a bath, and fell into bed. Exhausted from the flight, from the emotion that was tearing her apart, she slipped into a deep, unguarded sleep.

The nightmare invaded her dreams in the dark hours of night when she was too weak to fight it.

From the first moment she sensed there was something different to the familiar pattern. Tossing fitfully, she reluctantly allowed herself to be drawn along the pathway—not having a choice, but curious all the same.

Her heart thumped erratically as she watched the scene unfold—John finding the kink in the hose, herself on the phone and then scrambling up from the floor where she'd fallen.

Her gaze darted to the window, and the scene outside knocked the breath from her lungs. The wall of the shed was a sheet of flames, and she thought she could already see where it had burned a hole in the wood.

The gasoline!

She dropped the blanket and stumbled to the door, shoving it open. She screamed a warning.

John looked over his shoulder at her, and she began to run toward him when he didn't move away. She could see him more clearly as she closed the distance between them, worry drawing harsh lines in Hank's face—

"That's not right!" Sally bolted upright in bed. Tremors shook her body as she gulped over the sobs locked in her chest. "Hank wasn't even there," she whispered, rocking back and forth as confusion vied with terror. "It was John who died. Not Hank." Wide-eyed and terrified, she forced aside the visions of horror and comforted herself with the knowledge that she was awake.

It was over.

When she could do it without shaking, she leaned across to the bedside table and flicked on the light. And then, as she was taking a sip of water from the glass she'd left there, she realized something totally unprecedented had happened.

She'd awakened before the explosion . . . before anyone died.

That had never happened before. No matter how hard she'd tried to avoid it, she'd always been trapped within the cruel tentacles of her personal hell until the bitter end.

This time, though, Hank had been there, giving her the strength to stop when she needed it most. He'd helped her to do what she'd never been able to accomplish before.

He loved her. What a complete idiot she'd been not to take that love when it had been offered . . . to refuse to share her own in return. Alone. She'd thought that was the answer to an easier, *happier* life.

All because of a stupid dream.

Alone and content without Hank? The notion was ludicrous. She knew that now.

She was angry, but there was a method in her anger. The nightmare had controlled her for way too long. Its reign was over, she resolved, beginning tonight.

Gritting her teeth, she perceived that she had the edge. For the first time, she'd awakened before the end. All she had to do now was stop it before it got started.

A simple-enough task.

Dragging the bedclothes up to her shoulders, she reached for a tissue and swiped at her tears. Mind over matter, she told herself. She would conquer this thing, once and for all.

For herself . . . and for Hank. Her only regret was that she hadn't done it before she'd hurt him so badly.

Alone in a New York hotel room, far from home and the man she loved so dearly, her fears turning to shame, she calculated what she'd thrown away by being too afraid to live.

She would go back and beg for another chance. She'd chase him and plague him and do whatever she must to regain that which she'd so selfishly thrown away.

She loved him too much not to try.

Sally gave herself a week to conquer her fears. To do that, she dragged her past out into the open. All of the past, not just the tragedy that had made everything seem so worthless.

She spent the days working like a demon at the office while her nights were consumed with remembering each and every detail of her life with John. It was hard at first, particularly when she thought about the plans they'd made together—plans that had died with him.

She remembered the good times, something she'd never allowed herself to do before. It wasn't that she had ever begrudged those memories. Quite the contrary. Thinking of John had comforted her in those early days.

But then she'd realized that each and every memory eventually led to the end . . . a Technicolor explosion of hideous proportions. It hadn't been something she could face, not in the beginning.

The easy fix had been not to think about John at all. She'd blocked out conscious thought of the man she'd once loved, leaving only her unconscious mind to deal with the emotional backlash.

That was why the nightmares had stayed with her for so long. She saw that clearly. And when, after several nights during which she slept soundly and untroubled, she realized it had been herself she'd been fighting all along and not the nightmare.

It took remembering all the love she'd shared with John to make her realize she wouldn't have given that up, not for anything. The explosion had taken his life, but she still had the memories.

She tucked them into a corner of her heart and gathered her courage around her, not as a barrier but as support. The past was finally over. She was ready to live now, in the present, with all the excitement and joy that might bring. As for the future, well, she was learning to trust in that too.

It was a new person who checked out of the hotel a week later, a woman who was confident and whole and at peace with herself. On the plane west Sally fretted over the delays and wished she'd come back just one day sooner.

If she'd only gone back yesterday, she wouldn't be worrying today if Hank would ever forgive her her overwhelming stupidity, because she'd already know.

But she didn't. As Sally drove home along the back roads that skirted Oakville, she was so very afraid that he'd finally given up on Mad Sally. Holding Raspberry on her lap as she barreled along the rutted road that led to her property, she prayed he hadn't given up on Sally Michaels.

Thirteen

William Alton had a plan. He took a deep breath and wondered, not for the first time, if he was going to get away with it.

It didn't matter. Any risk was worth taking where his dad was concerned.

He stared at the house that stood silent and lifeless at the end of Blossom Lane and tried to put the events of the past several days in proportion. Sally had been gone for a week now. She'd missed the science fair at school on Tuesday night, and Willie hadn't felt any pleasure in the red ribbon he'd won. Awards night at the pizza place with the soccer team had been a dud without Sally to liven things up.

His dad had shown up in the dreaded tie. Sally wouldn't have let him wear a tie. Willie knew it. And his dad would have been smiling as though he meant it and not just because he had to.

Willie knew the difference, just as he knew what he had to do. He'd given it a lot of thought, holding long conversations with his mentor Doc Savage as he searched for the right thing to do.

The break had come through a buddy whose mother worked for a travel agent. Sally was due home today, sometime this afternoon.

That was why Willie was there. One foot on the ground, he sat on his bike and stared at the tree where it had all begun. He couldn't depend on Sally to come see his dad. He had to make his dad come to her.

Wheeling his bike over to the stone wall, Willie shrugged off his backpack and opened it. He pulled out the necessary materials and glanced up at the leafless crab-apple tree, reminding himself once again that it was for a good cause.

Then he unrolled a length of white toilet paper and went to work.

Willie drained the milk from his glass and wiped the white mustache off with his sleeve with impunity. His dad didn't notice, and his grandmother was too busy worrying about his dad to reprimand him. He sighed because he'd only done it to draw attention to himself.

He tried a more direct approach. "Last night was Halloween," he said.

Hank looked up, an apology in his eyes. "I had to work late. Sorry I missed seeing your costume."

"You didn't miss much," Willie said. "I wore my green sweats and went as a Ninja Turtle—along with half the other kids in town."

Hank just nodded and went back to pushing his dinner around his plate.

"We had nearly a hundred trick-or-treaters by here last night," Catherine said. "Did you have a good time with your friends, Willie?"

He shrugged. "It was okay. But I think I'm getting too old for this."

"What makes you say that, Willie?" Catherine asked.

He sighed heavily. "Sometimes the kids play tricks. It makes me uncomfortable."

She nodded. Hank sipped his coffee.

Drawing in a deep breath, Willie took the plunge. "I heard that a couple of kids went over to Mad Sally's and TP'd her crab-apple tree."

His dad's head jerked back up at that. "TP'd? What's that?"

"Toilet paper, Dad. Get with it. They threw rolls and rolls of the stuff all over her tree. It'll take her weeks to get it out."

Hank tossed his napkin onto the table. "Don't forget to finish your math homework," he said in his "Don't misunderstand what I'm saying" tone of voice.

Catherine looked faintly bemused as her son stormed out the door, wearing only a sweater against the evening chill. "Do you think he's going to fix the tree?" she asked her grandson.

"I think," Willie said, grinning, "he's going to get his tree fixed."

Sally cuddled Raspberry in her arms as she walked through the house and bade hello to her plants, all of which looked slightly the worse for wear. She promised each a drop or two of water the moment she had a free hand. Until she put down the rabbit, though, they'd have to wait. The pound or two Raspberry had lost over the past month hadn't exactly turned him into a featherweight.

Yawning away the remnants of her short nap, she tried valiantly to drag herself awake. The trip back from New York had been grueling, beginning with a takeoff delayed by weather and interrupted by an interminable stopover in Atlanta. She'd thought she was home free, though, when the plane had finally touched down at Stapleton International.

They'd had to wait nearly thirty minutes for a gate. All in all, she'd arrived three hours late and completely worn out.

Catching her reflection in the mirror, she briefly considered pulling herself together. While her jeans and cotton sweater were reasonably presentable, the rest of her looked a mess. Travel had definitely left its mark upon her normal postnap uglies. Wandering back into her bedroom, she discovered that her brush wasn't on the dresser. She sighed and remembered she hadn't unpacked before lying down for a quick snooze.

She retraced her steps to the living room, where she'd dumped her cases. Pausing to open the drapes, she was just about to put the rabbit on the floor when she glanced out the window and saw something in her tree. At least, she thought she did. Squinting, she forced her eyes to adjust to the dusky light of evening.

It moved!

Drawing an uneasy breath, she stared out the window at the apparition that crawled amid the leafless limbs and long sheets of white tissue. The toilet paper didn't bother her. That was almost a ritual for Mad Sally.

She just couldn't figure out why the trickster who'd put it there was still in her tree, this being the day after Halloween. Maybe he was caught in his own web, she mused. Then she saw a flash of silk.

"Raspberry," she said, her voice remarkably controlled, "how many people do we know who would wear Italian loafers and a tie when climbing a tree?"

The rabbit wiggled his butt and made it clear that he wanted to be let down. Sally complied, never taking her gaze off the tree.

"What the heck is Hank Alton doing up my tree?" she wondered aloud, the first real smile in a week curving her lips.

But at that precise moment the tree quivered and shook. *He'd lost his footing.*

Sally screamed.

Hank fell, hard, on his back. The air whooshed out of him and left him helpless.

He was thinking that Willie was going to have to get

another tree-climbing partner when his lungs began to fill with air. He was really getting too old for this, he mused, especially if he didn't know any better than to climb in his slick-soled loafers. Tentatively, he took one deep breath, then another, ready to laugh at his own stupidity when he had the resources. Then he heard a door slam.

Mad Sally! His limbs froze, and he squeezed his eyes shut. When had she come back? Why hadn't he realized she was in the house?

It didn't matter. Perhaps, if he stayed very still, she would come to him . . . and wouldn't go away. Maybe, just maybe, she'd take a chance and stay. The blood pounded in his ears as he lay there, helplessly awaiting his fate.

He expected no mercy.

He prayed for love.

He felt rather than heard her approach, the brush of cloth on his arm, the slight movement of the air that stirred with her arrival. He held his breath, afraid to look . . . afraid to see the absence of love in her eyes.

"Are you hurt?"

The soft voice surprised him, and he thought fleetingly that his worst fears hadn't come true at all. Her voice . . . Sally, his love, on her knees beside him, talking gently. It was as though she'd never spoken in anger, as though they'd never fought. But then he opened his eyes and saw the thing Willie had described.

It was Mad Sally in the flesh.

There could be no mistake about that. Her face was all squashed and wrinkled, and her hair stuck out all over. It was her eyes, though, that drew his gaze. Red-rimmed and almost colorless, they reminded him of the clearie marbles he'd bought Willie at the flea market.

With eyes like those, she had to be a witch.

He smiled.

Mad Sally lifted a hand toward him, and he knew she was going to do something simply wonderful . . . like turn him into a prince.

She slapped the side of his face. "Hank! Are you hurt? *Answer me*, dammit!" She slapped him again.

"Stop that!" He caught her hand in his. "I've heard of touching someone's life, but you're slapping mine right out my eardrums."

She looked relieved when he spoke, but her face was still ashen with concern. "Are you okay?"

"No." He shook his head against the hard ground. He'd never be okay until she agreed to marry him.

"What did you hurt?" she asked quickly, running her worried gaze down his supine body.

He groaned and rolled his eyes. "My pride. Should never have tried that in loafers."

"Did you break something?"

It finally occurred to him she wasn't hearing a word he said. He was just about to sit up and reassure her when she suddenly moved.

"You stay right there," she said, getting to her feet and racing toward the door. "I'll call emergency."

"*Wait!*"

Sally turned as a faint noise reached her ears. Hank was just a few steps behind her—upright and obviously in no pain at all.

"*You louse!*" she shouted. "*I thought you were hurt!*"

"*I said my pride hurt!*"

"You said what?" she asked with a giggle of disbelief.

Hank just sighed and raised his hand to flick the hair away from her ear. Then he gave her a meaningful look that she took to mean he might—but only *might*—have enough patience to wait for her to grab her hearing aids.

She dashed into the house and grabbed, her heart beating a different kind of rhythm now. Not panic, that was over. Not anger, although she should really take him to task for frightening her so. She was considering how she'd get back at him as she popped the second appliance into her ear, then sorted through her drawer for an old brush. She glanced in the mirror as she pulled it through her hair. She was beginning to look more like herself. The wrinkles and redness had nearly faded away.

Suddenly, a masculine roar of outrage reverberated through the house. She ran out to the front stoop where she'd left Hank.

"Damn rabbit!" he exclaimed, wounded disbelief in his voice as he bent over to check his ankle. "Did you train him to do that?"

"Do what?"

"Bite me!"

"Raspberry doesn't bite," she said, nevertheless eyeing the not-quite-lethargic movements of a suspiciously active rabbit. "Only young male rabbits bite, and that just when they're, well, agitated."

Hank watched the rabbit disappear into the maze at the side of the house. "I'd get a better book on rabbits, if I were you," he said at last, "because your little angel just took a wedge out of my ankle."

"Maybe he's agitated," she said.

He gave his ankle another rub and stood upright. "What does a rabbit have to be agitated about?"

"He's probably mad about being left at the vet for so long."

"And that's *my* fault?" he asked softly, lifting one hand to brush his knuckles across her cheek.

She shook her head, refusing to meet his eyes yet unwilling to lose the warmth of his touch. "No, it wasn't your fault." There was so much to say, and she didn't know where to begin. She didn't even know what he wanted to hear.

He made it easy. "I can't stop loving you just because you don't want me to," he said, cupping her chin with his fingers so that she had no choice but to look up at him.

All she saw in his eyes was love, and she understood then that it wouldn't go away without a fight.

She almost fainted with the relief that soared through her. "I don't want you to stop loving me," she finally said, holding his gaze with the strength she'd learned from him. "That's why I came back."

He nodded and touched her lips with his mouth . . . a rough, light caress that was the promise of heaven shared.

"Come sit under the tree," he suggested all of a sudden. "We can talk while I work. Is there anything in particular you want to say?"

Her heart jumped a couple of times before she answered. "Are you putting that stuff up or taking it down?"

He grinned. "Willie told me about what they'd done to your tree," he said as they crossed the lawn. "I didn't want you to come home to it."

"I would have been disappointed if they hadn't messed it up a bit," she said, shrugging aside his snort of disbelief as they stopped beneath the tree. "It's kind of a tradition."

He reached up to pull at a sheet of white. "Will you be here next year to find out if they do it again?"

She didn't answer. She couldn't. If she was in Oakville, she prayed that she would be with Hank and Willie and Catherine in the old Victorian.

Otherwise, she'd be gone.

Hank circled away in the silence that followed, coming back toward her a couple of minutes later as she was still struggling with her answer. She was shivering, he noticed, and he pulled off his sweater to tug it over her head.

Her face burrowed against the rough wool as she inhaled the scent of him. She had to tell him, she decided. Now, while he was still touching her, his hands tugging her hair free of the sweater, rolling up the sleeves.

He gave her confidence.

"If I could take back everything I said, I would do it," she said with total honesty. "My life before you was never your concern. I should have worked my own way through those problems long ago."

"Things don't work that way, love," he said gently, pulling her close against his chest.

"I didn't mean what I said last week—"

"Yes, you did." Holding her firmly, he leaned back against the mottled trunk. "You said it and you meant it."

She took a deep breath. "Everything's changed," she said, resting lightly against his lean, hard body. "I feel different from when I saw you last."

Hank took his time asking. "What has changed that's so important?"

"I slept for a whole week without the nightmare." It was a miracle, really. At least, after five long years, it seemed that way.

"Are you saying it's gone?"

Her heart skipped a beat, then settled as she realized who she was leaning on. Hank, with the enormous heart and patience of a saint. It would take that, at times.

"Sally?"

"Hmm?"

"Is the nightmare totally gone?" he asked again, his voice husky with some sort of emotion that was half pride and all love.

"I think so," she whispered. "But I've decided it doesn't matter one way or the other."

"Why?"

"Because I love you, and because I know that whatever happens, I don't want to miss out on the chance to be with you."

"You figured that out all on your own?" he asked softly.

She shook her head and touched her lips to his chin. "No. You were with me, beginning to end."

He understood, and it reassured him that he'd

been right to wait for her to come to her own sort of peace. "And now?"

"What?"

"If the nightmare comes back."

She swallowed hard. "If it comes back, I know you'll be there to help me through it."

"You should have known that last week," he said, and nibbled on her neck.

"If that was an 'I told you so,' I'll put a hex on you."

He just laughed and kissed her.

Beneath the autumn moon that rose slowly over a single crab-apple tree, a man held the woman he loved and shared a kiss of promise before leading her into the warmth of the house.

It was the last time they would sleep together in the house at the end of Blossom Lane. The next day, after a breathtakingly quick trip to Nevada, they returned to the ninety-year-old Victorian and together attempted to sneak upstairs past the boards that creaked.

Forewarned and forearmed, Willie and Catherine let loose a celebration from the upstairs landing, showering the newlyweds with numerous bags of confetti, until Hank and his bride were covered head to toe in the stuff.

They went on to bed in that condition, and it was days later when Hank asked Sally to wave her wand and get rid of it.

She just smiled and told him to do it himself.

Mad Sally was no more.

Epilogue

A cardboard box sat on the back porch. Willie had left it there, saying it was for old clothes and blankets. He was collecting things for the shelter just a couple blocks up from the soup kitchen in Denver.

Sally carefully folded the hooded cloak that had been so much a part of her life and placed it inside.

"You're sure about this?" Hank's voice came from over her shoulder.

She hadn't thought he was home. Edging backward until her back met the hard strength of his body, she relaxed in his embrace.

"I'm sure," she said softly. "It's part of me that doesn't exist anymore."

"Are you saying Mad Sally was a myth?"

She shook her head and leaned sideways so that her lips could find his.

"No, love," she said softly, touching his mouth with hers in quick, easy kisses. "Mad Sally was a *legend.*"

His laughter rumbled gently against her, and she retaliated by fastening her teeth on his lower lip.

Which was no punishment at all.

THE EDITOR'S CORNER

Next month LOVESWEPT celebrates heroes, those irresistible men who sweep us off our feet, who tantalize us with whispered endearments, and who challenge us with their teasing humor and hidden vulnerability. Whether they're sexy roughnecks or dashing sophisticates, dark and dangerous or blond and brash, these men are heartthrobs, the kind no woman can get enough of. And you can feast your eyes on six of them as they alone grace each of our truly special covers next month. HEARTTHROBS—heroes who'll leave you spellbound as only real men can.

Who better to lead our HEARTTHROBS lineup than Fayrene Preston and her hero, Max Hayden, in **A MAGNIFICENT AFFAIR**, LOVESWEPT #528? Max is the best kind of kisser: a man who takes his time and takes a woman's breath away. And when Ashley Whitfield crashes her car into his seaside inn, he senses she's one sweet temptation he could go on kissing forever. But Ashley has made a habit of drifting through her life, and it'll take all of Max's best moves to keep her in his arms for good. A magnificent love story, by one of the best in the genre.

The utterly delightful **CALL ME SIN**, LOVESWEPT #529, by award-winner Jan Hudson, will have you going wild over Ross Berringer, a Texas Ranger as long and as tall as his twin brother, Holt, who thrilled readers in **BIG AND BRIGHT**, LOVESWEPT #464. The fun in **CALL ME SIN** begins when handsome hunk Ross moves in next door to Susan Sinclair. He's the excitement the prim bookstore owner has been missing in her life—and the perfect partner to help her track down a con artist. But once Ross's downright neighborly attention turns Susan inside out with ecstasy, she starts running scared. How Ross unravels her intriguing mix of passion and fear is a sinfully delicious story you'll want to read.

Doris Parmett outdoes herself in creating a perfect HEARTTHROB in **MR. PERFECT**, LOVESWEPT #530. Chase Rayburn is the epitome of sex appeal, a confirmed bachelor who can charm a lady's socks off—and then all the rest of her clothes. So why does he feel wildly jealous over Sloan McKay's personal ad on a billboard? He's always been close to his law partner's widow and young son, but he's never before wanted to kiss Sloan until she melted with wanton pleasure. Shocking desire, daring seduction, and a friend-ship that deepens into love—a breathtaking combination in one terrific book.

Dangerously sexy, his gaze full of delicious promises, Hunter Kincaid will have you dreaming of **LOVE AND A BLUE-EYED COWBOY,** LOVESWEPT #531, by Sandra Chastain. Hunter knows he can win the top prize in a motorcycle scavenger hunt, but he doesn't count on being partnered with petite, smart-mouthed Fortune Dagosta. A past sorrow has hardened Hunter's heart, and the last person he wants for a companion for a week is a beautiful woman whose compassion is easily aroused and whose body is made for loving. Humorous and poignant, the sensual adventure that follows is a real winner!

Imagine a man who has muscles like boulders and a smoky drawl that conjures up images of rumpled sheets and long, deep kisses—that's Storm Dalton, Tami Hoag's hero in **TAKEN BY STORM,** LOVESWEPT #532. A man like that gets what he wants, and what he wants is Julia McCarver. But he's broken her heart more than once, and she has no intention of giving him another chance. Years of being a winning quarterback has taught Storm ways to claim victory, and the way he courts Julia is a thrilling and funny romance that'll keep you turning the pages.

Please give a rousing welcome to new author Linda Warren and her first LOVESWEPT, **BRANDED,** #532, a vibrantly emotional romance that has for a hero one of the most virile rodeo cowboys ever. Tanner Danielson has one rule in life: Never touch another man's wife. And though he wanted Julie Fielding from the first time he saw her, he never tasted her fire because she belonged to another. But now she's free and he isn't waiting a moment longer. A breathlessly exciting love story with all the wonderfully evocative writing that Linda displayed in her previous romances.

On sale this month from FANFARE are three marvelous novels. **LIGHTS ALONG THE SHORE,** by immensely talented first-time author Diane Austell, is set in nineteenth-century California, and as the dramatic events of that fascinating period unfold, beautiful, impetuous Marin Gentry must face up to the challenges in her turbulent life, including tangling with notorious Vail Severance. Highly acclaimed Patricia Potter delivers **LAWLESS,** a poignant historical romance about a schoolteacher who longs for passionate love and finds her dreams answered by a coldhearted gunfighter who's been hired to drive her off her land. In **HIGHLAND REBEL,** beloved author Stephanie Bartlett whisks you away to the rolling hills and misty valleys of the Isle of Skye, where proud highland beauty Catriona Galbraith is fighting for her land and her people, and where bold Texas rancher Ian MacLeod has sworn to win her love.

Also available this month in the hardcover edition from Doubleday (and in paperback from FANFARE in March) is **LUCKY'S LADY** by ever-popular LOVESWEPT author Tami Hoag. Those of you who were enthralled with the Cajun rogue Remy Doucet in **THE RESTLESS HEART,** LOVESWEPT #458, will find yourself saying Ooh la la when you meet his brother, Lucky, for he is one rough and rugged man of the bayou. And when he takes the elegent Serena Sheridan through a Louisiana swamp to find her grandfather, they generate what *Romantic Times* has described as "enough steam heat to fog up any reader's glasses."

Happy reading!

With warmest wishes,

Nita Taublib

Nita Taublib
Associate Publisher/LOVESWEPT
Publishing Associate/FANFARE

FANFARE

ILLUSION

by Paula Volsky

In a world where magic determines birthright, spoiled nobleman's daughter Eliste vo Derrivale hopes to be presented to the king at the dazzling court in Sherreen. She leaves behind her love for a man whom by law she can never marry, and takes the chance to pursue her dream -- a dream abruptly shattered by the violent revolution that tears her world apart. It's a rebellion that could bring her the love she desires. But first, like the peasants she disdained, she must scramble for bread in the streets of the city, orphaned and outlawed by the new regime. At the height of her despair, she finds the man she long ago left behind and together, in a country wracked with change, they must find a way to survive in a world gone mad . . . with liberty.

Magic: it's pure illusi

ILLUSIO

it's pure m